VAGABOND NURSE

Whilst taking a locum in Casualty at St. Anne's Infirmary, Nurse Liza Carter is disappointed to find that there are no vacant posts in an overseas Community Health project with Dr. Andrew Peterson. Reluctantly, she finds herself attracted to the young doctor, but he seems to have eyes only for tall, aristocratic-looking medical student Martha Newman, who makes it plain to all that he is her property.

ANN JONES

VAGABOND NURSE

Complete and Unabridged

LINFORD
Leicester

First published in Great Britain

First Linford Edition
published October 1994

British Library CIP Data

Jones, Ann
   Vagabond nurse.—Large print ed.—
Linford romance library
I. Title II. Series
813.54 [F]

ISBN 0-7089-7608-5

Published by
F. A. Thorpe (Publishing) Ltd.
Anstey, Leicestershire

Set by Words & Graphics Ltd.
Anstey, Leicestershire
Printed and bound in Great Britain by
T. J. Press (Padstow) Ltd., Padstow, Cornwall

This book is printed on acid-free paper

1

NURSE LIZA CARTER ran down the steps of the Nurses' Residence, raced a bus to the stop in front of St. Anne's Infirmary and leaped aboard as it pulled away. Her green eyes sparkled with excitement.

A half hour later, wind-blown and out of breath, she entered the outer office of United Aid International.

The place was empty. She flung her coat over a chair, ran her fingers through her long unruly curls and glanced at her watch. She was early. Too keyed up and restless to sit still, she crossed the room to peer at a huge map of Asia.

Standing on tiptoe, she found the main route into the Province of Assam. As her finger traced the thin black line twisting north from the Pakistan border toward the city of Gauhati, she was aware someone had entered the room. But all her attention was focused on the city beside the Brahmaputra River toward which her finger moved.

A bright overhead light was switched on, casting the shadow of Liza's slim figure across the map.

"You're heading for Gauhati?" The speaker's voice was deep and resonant.

Keeping one finger on the map, Liza half turned to face the man who stood smiling down at her.

"I hope so. I mean . . . Yes, I am."

"So, you must be Nurse Carter."

She looked into the bluest eyes she'd ever seen, or as she later told her friend, Clare Robson, she fell into them and drowned.

"But how on earth do you know who I am?"

"I know all about you, Nurse Carter."

Liza noticed a teasing gleam in his eye as he continued.

"After all, I'll be travelling to Assam

with you. Since we'll be living in an extremely isolated situation, I've been anxious, naturally, to learn what I could . . . "

Seeing her confusion, he dropped his half joking tone. "I'm Andrew Peterson. Hasn't anyone told you I've been assigned to the community health project? We'll be working together out there."

For a moment Liza was too flustered to notice his hand outstretched to shake hers. She'd been told nothing about him. Yet, the name Andrew Peterson rang a bell, and she was sure she'd seen him before. She noted his strong, craggy features, deeply tanned and softened by the warmth of those astonishing blue eyes and his gentle, almost playful smile. A long scar crossed the right side of his forehead. He was not a man she would forget.

"You don't work at St. Anne's Infirmary, do you? I don't think we've met before?"

He looked at her quizzically. "I'd

most certainly remember if we'd met. I'm sure I've never had that pleasure."

Liza blushed as he gazed at her with open admiration.

He said, "I don't work at St. Anne's; although I was a houseman there five or six years ago. That's where you work, right?"

She nodded. "I'm doing a locum in Casualty, just 'til I leave for Assam."

Andrew Peterson grinned. "So, one way or another, we were destined to meet. I was also offered a locum there — to fill in until my marching orders came. St. Anne's must be holding pen for medical missionaries."

Liza sighed, "I've been waiting months, but I have a feeling the waiting is over. Otherwise why would we be here today? I think we're here to pick up our plane tickets. Have you heard anything?" Mischievously, she added, "Aside from all the things you heard about me, that is."

Her question went unanswered. Dr. Kingsley, the Board Chairman, himself, summoned them into the Director's office, saying, "Liza, my dear, you are good to come on such short notice. You've met Dr. Peterson?"

"Yes, just now." Of course, he'd be a doctor, she thought.

"And Andrew, it's good to see you've recovered from your ordeal."

For a moment Liza wondered what ordeal. But her curiosity about the purpose of their meeting drove out all other questions. They followed Dr. Kingsley into a large, cluttered office that smelled of pipe tobacco.

A half hour later Liza stood again in front of the huge map. Now she gazed through a mist of unshed tears at the tiny kingdom in the Himalayas that had been the centre of her universe for so long. Her cherished dream of working there was shattered. Neither she nor Dr. Peterson, nor anyone else would be needed in Assam. The mission her grandmother had founded there fifty years before was to be closed.

"It's very sudden, I know," Dr.

Kingsley had said. "And I'm afraid there are no other posts vacant at present. There's work to be done, but no money."

The elderly Doctor who had known Liza's grandmother and had been so encouraging and helpful when Liza had first applied for her position fully realized what a blow his news would be to the young nurse.

"We wish it were possible to carry on, but we have been asked to leave so we must go."

He had explained how political changes in the region effected aid programmes, but Liza took in only half what he said. She had come, believing she'd be given her departure date, and when she thought she'd be working with Dr. Peterson, her heart had turned somersaults. I should have known it was too good to be true, she thought.

"Are you coming, Nurse Carter?" Dr. Peterson stood with his hand on the doorknob, waiting.

6

Liza shook her head. She needed time to pull herself together. "In a few minutes. Goodbye, Dr. Peterson."

He left, but moments later he was back. "Food always helps. Take my word for it. Come along. I know just the thing."

He gave her no choice, bundling her into her coat, hurrying her along to Covent Garden at a pace that allowed for no conversation. He settled her on a bench and fetched steamy coffee and two gargantuan slices of Black Forest gateau. She opened her mouth to speak, but he said, "Eat first."

He kept glancing at her, as though to see that she was enjoying her cake properly. She was, indeed, having skipped lunch. She was unaware of a dab of chocolate on her chin, and he found this strangely touching. Her copper-coloured curls were awry and she brushed them back impatiently. Her nose was red from the cold. All together, she looked way too young, at the moment, to be alone on the streets of London, never mind Gauhati.

When every last crumb was consumed, he smiled at her and said, "Now, you were about to say . . . ?"

Liza laughed. "Thank you, that was delicious. And please forgive me for being weepy. I expect you are as disappointed as I am that the mission closed."

She wondered if he had a wife and family to think of. He looked thirtyish but, somehow, he didn't have a married look. And it was unlikely anyone would take a family to Assam.

He was thoughtful a long moment. "It's a little different for me. I've been away five years and this might be a good time to leave overseas work. It might be very pleasant, settling down in England."

Liza caught her breath and was about to speak, but she gazed at him half wistfully and said nothing.

He continued, "I didn't have the same strong commitment to the Assam project that you had. Yet, I can't honestly say I feel sorry you won't be going."

Puzzled, she waited to hear why, but he seemed lost in thought and when she finally asked him why, he was evasive. "Those kind of places can be pretty rough."

She wondered again about the 'ordeal' Dr. Kingsley mentioned. Had some bad experience turned him against mission work? He wouldn't have had to worry about Assam. When her grandmother had to retire, she left with great reluctance. She'd been delighted Liza wanted to continue what she had begun. She'd never worried that it might be too rough.

As though he could read her thoughts, Dr. Peterson remarked that much of the Third World was greatly changed since her grandmother's time. "I don't think it's the best place for a girl like you."

"What absolute nonsense!"

Her vehemence didn't seem to surprise him. He moved their cake plates aside and leaning toward her, he said very seriously, "I'm sure it would be an insult to your intelligence if I reminded you that right here in London . . . "

"I know! I know!" Liza broke in. "Right here in London there is enough suffering to keep us busy all our lives. Those may not be the exact words you'd use, but . . . "

"They're close enough. Of course the remark is trite, but no less valid. I understand your feelings about a mission founded by your grandmother. I do sympathize."

Liza spoke earnestly, hoping she could make him understand. "The difference between the misery in London and that in Assam is that in London we know someone will try to do something about it."

"Because there are people like you to do it." Dr. Peterson tapped the table top for emphasis. He leaned back and smiled, satisfied that his logic had triumphed.

This was the same argument Liza

and her friend Clare had gone through over and over. She was tired of it and in no mood to defend her point with Dr. Peterson. He was so nice, but very clearly an over-protective male.

"What about you," she asked. "Do you have any interesting alternatives?"

"I need some time to think. That locum at St. Anne's might be just the thing for a month or so."

Liza's heart leaped. She would see him again. But the thought of St. Anne's brought her to her feet. A swift glance at her watch confirmed what she feared. The afternoon was nearly gone. She'd have hardly any sleep before going on night duty.

They walked to the underground, hurrying again — too fast to chat. Liza noticed Dr. Peterson's effect on women they met along the way. Their admiration was clearly evident. It would be enough to make a man conceited, she thought, and yet he showed no signs of conceit. He was self-assured, but she liked that.

As they parted at the underground, she told him, in her forthright way, "You're the only nice thing that happened today."

He smiled and gave her a quick little hug. "That's what I was thinking about you."

Back at the Nurses Residence she figured if she skipped tea she could sleep four hours before going on duty. But sleep would not come.

Her thoughts kept returning to Dr. Peterson. She visualized his face and again felt she had seen him somewhere before, and not long ago. Trying to remember when and where, she finally fell asleep a half hour before her alarm went off.

Dr. Peterson walked back into her life three nights later, and Sister Clare Robson cleared up the mystery of where Liza had seen his face before.

"On the six o'clock news in my flat, Liza. Don't you remember?"

"On television? No, I don't know what you're talking about."

Clare lowered her voice as the Paediatric Consultant walked past the nurses' station.

"Dr. Andrew Peterson is the man who rescued all those patients single handed . . . and was nearly killed."

"Of course!" Liza exclaimed. "When that jungle hospital was attacked somewhere in Africa! I knew I had seen him . . . "

Dr. Peterson had appeared in Casualty a few hours before while the Day Sister was handing over. When she introduced him as the locum for Dr. Hopkins, he winked at Liza, who blushed crimson. This was noted with great interest by the rest of the staff.

He was friendly but a bit more formal as he shook hands with Clare and old Nurse Daniels and the student nurse who seemed suddenly paralyzed. Then he turned to Liza and his smile broadened.

"We've met. How are you, Nurse Carter?"

She murmured, "Fine," but she

thought 'in shock' would be nearer the truth. She had never really believed he would turn up at St. Anne's, and here he was in her own department. With everyone standing around, she didn't know how to respond to him.

Feeling she mustn't act too familiar, she quickly excused herself to start her night's work. She knew it would be Clare, as Night Sister in charge, who would get to show him around. She wished she could do it, but she was soon too busy with an overdose patient to think of anything else.

On her break, when she and Clare entered the staff canteen, she felt an under-current of barely suppressed excitement in the atmosphere.

The focus of everyone's attention seemed to be the couple seated in a corner beyond the battery of snack-dispensing machines that hummed and flickered along the walls.

Liza recognized Martha Newman, the medical student who had recently started her six week surgery module.

She was leaning across a small red plastic table toward Dr. Peterson. Her long, honey-coloured hair hung forward, half hiding her profile.

Liza felt irrationally peeved at the sight of Dr. Peterson, listening so intently to her monologue. She reckoned from the many furtive glances in their direction that most people had heard already about the new doctor's African adventures.

But what was Martha Newman's connection? They were obviously not strangers to each other.

"She knew him from somewhere," Clare explained to Liza. "Actually, she's the one who reminded me he was the doctor we saw on TV, though I think I'd have recognized him. She's been telling everybody."

"She doesn't usually have that much to say," Liza observed.

Clare agreed. "But she's certainly worked up about this."

"So is everybody else."

"Don't look at them," Clare ordered.

"How impolite people are to gape at a new-comer. Though I must admit, he's quite extra-ordinary to look at."

"It's that sun tan and those eyes, I suppose," Liza observed as she drew her cup of machine coffee.

Clare led the way to a table, saying, "Come on, we have other things to talk about. What's new with the job search? Is anything good turning up?"

Liza sat where she could glance, now and then, at the table in the corner. Clare had to repeat her question.

"I still have no idea where I'm going," Liza admitted. "It will take a while to get answers to my applications. Will you take me in if I wind up home-less next month?"

She meant to be joking, and when Clare took her seriously and said of course she would take her in, it gave her little comfort. She couldn't imagine Clare, herself, ever being in such a spot.

She glanced at her friend's serene, madonna-like face. It was framed by smooth, sable-coloured hair pulled back in a neat chignon, a face that expressed calm competence.

Clare always had things under control. She was happily settled in her career, she had bought a flat, and she was engaged to Simon Crawford, a most eligible bachelor.

And I'm still floundering around, Liza thought.

Clare said, "I wish you'd take a permanent post here. I'll miss you terribly after all our years together."

"No, you won't. You'll have Simon."

"True, and you, silly goose, want to leave just when God's other gift to women arrives at St. Anne's." She nodded toward Dr. Peterson.

"And walks straight into the waiting arms of Martha Newman," Liza muttered.

2

LIZA looked up from the case sheet she was hurriedly filling a fortnight later. "Good Heavens, it's Friday the thirteenth!"

Clare called over her shoulder, "That might account for the chaos around here."

"But the thirteenth is always lucky for me."

"Proof that you're a witch," said the houseman, glumly hurrying past.

Looking around her, she had to admit a lot of people had found the day anything but auspicious. But I need a change of luck so badly, she thought. Nothing is going right.

Clare was back to snatch a handful of records. "If you get a free minute, can we have a word? It's urgent."

Since Clare tended toward understatement, her 'urgent' could mean positively desperate.

Liza was far too busy to worry about it. The registrar from Ear, Nose and Throat had handed her a screaming two-year-old.

"Don't try to reason with him, just hold him still," he commanded.

He was exploring for three red beads the mother insisted had disappeared up her child's nose. He didn't hide his impatience with the lusty little boy, and Liza didn't blame the child for objecting.

Dr. Peterson put his head out of a cubicle and beckoned to her. "Where's Nurse Daniels? She can hold that child. I need you in here, Nurse Carter."

The registrar answered for her. "Nurse Daniels is taking a patient to Maternity."

"Don't we have a medical student somewhere?" the doctor asked.

He knows very well we do, Liza thought. I saw him driving her to work.

The registrar sounded put-upon.

"Yes, but everyone's busy. If you need Nurse Carter, I'll get the child's mother to hold him."

"No, carry on. I can wait," said Dr. Peterson.

But the registrar walked away, muttering about the uselessness of hysterical parents.

Alone with the patient, Liza calmed him by offering a ring of keys from her pocket.

"What do you have in your pocket?" she asked.

He thought this over, reached deep into his pants pocket, then opened his fat little fist, solemnly displaying three red beads.

Somewhere behind her, Liza heard a hoot of laughter from Dr. Peterson.

Receiving the beads and her little boy separately, the mother broke down, sobbing with relief and needed comforting.

So it went, all evening — one crisis after another.

When Liza finally got back to

Clare, her friend whispered, "Has Dr. Peterson said anything to you yet?"

"Nothing you could call meaningful."

"He hasn't spoken to you about a job?"

The word job had an electrifying effect on Liza. "What job?"

"I don't know what job, but I've been afraid you'd accept some other offer. You haven't, have you?"

"I've been sleeping. After last night — six admissions, you may remember."

"Yes, but I know you've been hounding the registry nearly every day since . . . "

"Well, the result has been absolute nil. What did Dr. Peterson say? Don't torture me!"

"If only you hadn't left in such a rush this morning. I had the impression Dr. Peterson wants somebody to work with him abroad."

Liza was speechless a full sixty seconds. "I don't believe it. My luck must be changing. That would be heaven on earth. What did he say? Please, Clare! Tell me his exact words."

Before Clare could answer, Nurse Daniels, appeared. "Dr. Peterson wants Nurse Carter in room three, please."

"Maybe now he'll tell you himself . . . " Clare began; but Liza was already heading toward the treatment room.

I could leave tomorrow, she thought. She had made a point of avoiding long contracts; her worldly goods were limited to what she could carry; and her passport and immunizations were up to date. She could be on the next flight to . . .

She had to force herself back to earth when someone behind her said, "Excuse me, Nurse Carter."

She stood aside while a junior nurse wheeled in a trolley of instruments and a suture set. Before following her, she glanced back at Clare who winked encouragingly.

Liza shook her head. It was unlikely

that Dr. Peterson would mention the job or anything else while they were with a patient.

It was odd that he had talked to Clare instead of speaking directly to her. They were thrown together often in the course of their work, even though he spent any free moments with Martha Newman.

As she entered the treatment room, Dr. Peterson looked up, then went on removing a mass of bloody dressings from his patient's head and face. The patient had been in a road accident and had put his head through the windscreen.

"Start a drip, please, Nurse Carter, and we'll want five milligrams of diazapam intravenously."

While she carried out his orders, the doctor reassured his patient.

"We'll be working an hour or more, but we'll give you something to make you drowsy, and if you fall asleep, so much the better."

He discarded his soiled rubber gloves,

scrubbed again and held out his hands for her to help him into new ones. The room was hot, and he asked her to swab the perspiration from his forehead. As she performed this intimate task, his eyes held hers, and she felt her face flush.

They returned to their patient, and removed the final layer of dressings.

Liza prepared to assist with the suturing.

Half way along, the doctor straightened and stretched. He looked across the sleeping patient and asked, "How did you know the beads were in his pocket?"

When Liza finally realized what he was talking about, she laughed.

"I know about boy's pockets. They're always full of odd things. And besides, would you put beads in your nose if you had pockets?"

He bent over his work again. "It sounds like you've had a lot of experience with boys."

"I have."

"Younger brothers?"

"No, older boys mostly. Not brothers: I'm an only child."

Seeing the doctor's raised eyebrows, she explained. "I grew up in a boy's boarding school . . . "

The eyebrows climbed higher.

"Where my father was headmaster," she quickly added.

"Which school?"

"Willowbrook, in Cumbria."

He signalled for her to adjust the light, then he said, "Near Carlisle? We beat you every year at rugby."

"You must have been at Deanchester!"

He nodded. "Cumbria is my idea of heaven, especially the Lake District this time of year. Have you been back lately?"

Liza knew exactly how long it had been. Her father's funeral was eighteen months ago. "I hardly ever go back," she answered. "My family isn't there now. Do you go back?"

"I'm heading north about two minutes after we go off duty."

They were nearly finished when Dr. Peterson said, "You'd make an excellent theatre nurse. Have you thought of doing that kind of work . . . now that your original plans are changed?"

She hesitated, wondering if the question had something to do with a job he had in mind for her. She said, "Not specifically. I'm most concerned about where I work."

He looked up. "Oh yes. I remember."

She said, "Cumbria is all I've seen of the world, except for London, of course, and Scotland where my grandparents lived. I'd still like to work in a really interesting place."

"Interesting how? Exotic, romantic . . . that sort of thing?" His tone seemed disapproving.

"At least new and different from any place I've been."

"Istanbul, Nairobi, Budapest?"

"Any or all of those would do fine," she laughed. "Or Bangkok, Katmandu or Baghdad." To Liza, these weren't just place names, they were poetry.

"And what's wrong with Cumbria?"

"It's lovely, but completely familiar."

"Well, for the moment, we'd better have another blood pressure reading, Nurse Carter."

They finished in silence. Dr. Peterson sent Liza for the porter to take the patient to intensive care.

She was pleasantly surprised to find the waiting room empty.

"That's all for tonight," Clare called from her office.

"Ha!" exclaimed the doctor cynically. He picked up Clare's phone. Liza heard him tell the switchboard he'd be in his room.

Her mood of happy expectation changed to disappointment when he thanked her, as usual, for her 'exemplary assistance', yawned and strolled off down the corridor.

When the lift door closed behind him, Clare said, "Tell me quickly. What did he say about the job."

"You tell me," Liza replied bitterly.

"You're the only one who has anything to tell."

"You mean he didn't say anything about working with him?"

"Not a word."

"How weird! I wish you had been here this morning when he took that phone call. He seemed so anxious to talk to you."

"What phone call?" Liza begged her friend to begin at the beginning.

She was afraid she'd find Clare had misunderstood whatever the doctor had said. Yet, there had to be some explanation for his unusually chummy manner toward her tonight.

"Start where he comes up to you and says, Hello, Sister Robson."

"He didn't, actually. What happened was that I called him to the phone for an overseas call. I think it was from Paris, He took it at my desk."

"Clare! You wouldn't eavesdrop!"

Clare's tone was indignant. "Of course not on purpose. In fact, I started to leave so he would have

28

privacy, but he told me not to go; he would only be a minute. His caller did most of the talking, anyway. I had the feeling it was good news."

Clare thought a minute, frown lines creasing her pretty brow, as she tried to remember exactly what had been said.

"He must have been talking about you. He said, 'You'll like her. She's bright and energetic and pleasant'."

Liza couldn't hide her dismay. "So, from this phone call you overheard, you leap to the conclusion that he was talking about me and wants me to work with him! Oh, Clare!"

"Hold on. Let me finish. After he hung up he just stood here smiling. Finally, he sat down to write something in his diary. I was finished by then and about to leave. He asked if you'd already gone."

"I must have just missed him," Liza moaned.

"Then he asked if I knew when your locum ends. Is it three weeks from now?"

"About that."

"Well, I said about three, and he said, 'Good, that will work out well enough, unless she already has a job'."

"That does sound hopeful." Liza smiled at her friend, regretting her impatience.

"As I left, he was sitting here, as though waiting in case you were still around."

Someone walked by in the corridor and the two nurses lowered their voices. Liza said, "Surely, he told you something about the job — what country it's in . . . "

Clare patted her hand. "Liza, dear, he didn't tell me another thing, but as I said, I understood the call was from Paris. I thought he would be talking to you about it as soon as he saw you again."

Liza slumped in her chair. Why hadn't he said anything? He had, in fact, mentioned working as a theatre nurse. And she'd implied she'd do anything, but not in Cumbria. How did Paris fit into the picture. Maybe he was going to a French colony.

"Has he ever said anything to you about his plans?" Liza asked.

Clare said they'd never had time to chat. She looked for her pen and pulled a pile of papers toward herself. Liza would ordinarily recognize this as body language for let's-get-to-work, but she was lost in thought.

After several minutes, she looked at Clare with shining eyes and said, "Wouldn't it be absolute paradise — working in some far off place with Dr. Peterson?"

"That might be Paradise for you," Clare laughed. "I'll take my sweet Simon Crawford and my Victorian flat, thank you all the same. And remember, you can't leave the country until after our wedding, so keep your dates straight."

Clare kept at her paper work while Liza got them coffee from the machine in the waiting room. The night was unseasonably warm for April, and someone had hooked the doors open. The bosky smell of springtime merged with sharper hospital smells. When a breeze sprang up and ruffled notices on the bulletin board, Liza went, reluctantly, to close the doors.

Returning, she found Martha Newman leaning over the desk speaking to Clare in a whisper. She noticed how the strip light gleamed on Martha's smooth light brown hair.

If only her own hair would lie flat and sleek like that, instead of kinking into ringlets. And if only her own eyes were big and blue and dramatic like Martha's instead of green. She supposed a tall, aristocratic-looking girl like Martha would be irresistible to men. She certainly seemed to have Dr. Peterson under her spell.

Liza waited by the doorway until she left. When she sat down again to finish her coffee, Clare said, "She's going to bed and doesn't want to be called unless it's urgent. She said she has a big day tomorrow."

Liza, idly swirling coffee in the bottom of her cup, noticed it was eleven. The electric wall clock made the only sound in the overheated room. The big hand moved in noisy jerks, and listening to the splotch of used-up minutes, she felt a desperate urgency to get on with the career she had planned.

Clare gave her a look that clearly said, there's work to be done. She rose, put their paper cups in the bin, and went to check that the junior nurse had left the treatment room in proper order.

When Liza returned from her rounds of patients being kept in Casualty overnight, Clare said, "We've been alerted to expect an accident victim arriving shortly by ambulance."

Liza heard her call Dr. Peterson. She had just put down the phone when they heard the ambulance arrive. Since the porter was on his break, Liza went to hold the doors, but before she reached them, the ambulance attendant burst in calling for a doctor.

"I'm afraid the patient's died!"

She went out with him. As he and the driver wheeled the old man in, she walked beside him, feeling vainly for a pulse. She put her stethoscope to his chest, but heard nothing. She was fastening the blood pressure cuff when she heard running footsteps. Then Dr. Peterson was there.

The ambulance attendant looked up, saying, "He's dead, Doctor. He was all right a few minutes ago."

"What happened?" Dr. Peterson was already examining the patient for signs of life.

The ambulance driver reported he'd been found unconscious, apparently knocked out from a fall.

"But he was awake when we picked him up, and he said he was all right. He didn't even want to come along in the ambulance, but he was short of breath and wheezy."

Standing back now that the doctor had taken over, Liza sadly observed that the old man had obviously been very much alive and busy a short time ago. A metal tape measure and a tide table had fallen onto the trolley from his overall pocket. There was fresh blue paint on his sleeve. It had smeared her uniform when she felt for his pulse. He looked to be in his sixties, round-faced and nice looking, but scruffy. She felt a surge of grief for him.

Clare had called the registrar and the new houseman, who looked at the patient and asked, "Dead on arrival?"

"Not necessarily," Dr. Peterson said. "Get the defibrillator cart and the ECG."

The houseman shrugged and started toward the office.

"On the double," Dr. Peterson snapped.

As they worked Liza glanced at the oscilloscope. The picture could be worse. Instead of the flat line indicating a lifeless heart, it showed the irregular peaks of a heart shuddering in useless fibrillation.

Clare had called in an anaesthetist to force respiration and monitor the electrocardiograph.

"I'm afraid you're looking for a miracle," he muttered to Dr. Peterson, who muttered back, "Okay, why not?"

He looked for Liza. "Is there a femoral pulse, Nurse?"

As she moved the patient's leg to get at the large artery in his groin, a pair of pliers clattered onto the tile floor, followed by a miniature hailstorm of brass rivets, dribbling from the old man's trouser pocket.

"This gentleman was obviously not ready to pack it in," said the doctor as he kicked the hardware aside.

Liza reported a femoral pulse.

"Good, Nurse Carter." The doctor smiled at her; then patted the anaesthetist's shoulder. "You're doing nicely. Look, he's getting back some colour."

For the first time, the team shared Dr. Peterson's belief — there might be some hope. But hope faded when, in spite of strong shocks, the heart continued to fibrillate. The anaesthetist shook his head. "I'm afraid he's had it."

Ignoring him, Dr. Peterson picked up the electrodes and nodded to the registrar. "Okay, higher voltage again."

Liza held her breath, knowing they couldn't go on giving these strong shocks, for each one resulted in cell damage. But Dr. Peterson grimly carried on.

Liza heard a gasp of amazement from the anaesthetist and looked up at the screen. She saw that the patient's heart had ceased its fluttering. It had begun to beat on its own.

The houseman said, "I wouldn't believe this if I hadn't seen it."

"Let's get a drip going," Dr. Peterson said, with a note of pure relief in his voice. He discovered Liza standing beside him, ready to do just that.

"Nurse Carter!" he exclaimed. "Did you know all along he would live?"

Liza just smiled.

"We'll get him up to the Coronary

Care Unit," Dr. Peterson said.

A few minutes later, as Liza and the porter wheeled the patient into the lift, the doctor joined them.

The gate clattered shut, and the patient opened his eyes. The light made him blink, but he glanced around until he found Liza and Dr. Peterson. He gazed at the smiling couple a long moment before closing his eyes again.

Clare and a junior nurse were alone when Liza returned to Casualty. The two friends grinned happily at each other. Winning such a dramatic life-or-death struggle left them both feeling too high to easily settle back to work. Liza hummed as she helped the junior clear up the mess left in the corridor where Dr. Peterson had encountered his patient. The junior held up a pair of greasy pliers.

"What did you use these for?"

"Do you mean you haven't been taught to use them?" she replied, leaving the girl's curiosity unsatisfied, but sending Clare into a fit of giggles.

She looked around for the rivets and found them scattered under a radiator. A soiled and wrinkled piece of notebook paper lay beside them. She smoothed it and saw the day's date at the top of a list:

check bilge pump
varnish mast
buy blue paint

She needed to read no further to know the list belonged with the pliers and rivets. She had suspected, when she'd seen the tide table fall from his pocket that the old man had been working on a boat.

She felt a twinge of guilt about reading his private papers and quickly took her little collection along to be stored with the rest of his property until he was ready to go home. Then she stepped outside for a breath of air.

She leaned against a pillar, listening to the night murmur of the city, watching a flimsy cloud cross the moon. A glow of satisfaction had replaced the vague discontent she had been feeling in recent weeks.

I agonize about the past and future too much, she thought. The present is full of good things — the balmy night, their success in reviving the old man, and the new friendliness of Dr. Peterson, regardless of its cause.

She heard Clare tell someone she'd gone out, and reluctantly she started back inside.

The door swung open before her, and the man she'd been thinking of said, "Beware, Nurse Carter! There's madness in moonlight, you know."

"So that's what's been doing it," she laughed, and continued on her way inside as the doctor went to lean against the pillar she had just left.

"Stay a minute," he said.

Now, she thought, at last, he's going to tell me about the job. She'd rather be sitting across a desk. This was not a very business-like setting.

"Tell me about being the only girl

at Willowbrook," he said, throwing her thoughts into disarray.

"It was fun," she managed. "But I wasn't the only girl. Sister Robson was there, too. Her father was the History Master. But she was three years ahead of me; and later she was sent off to a girl's school."

"Leaving you to be the most popular girl in the county, no doubt."

Liza smiled but said nothing. Let him think that, if he'd like. No use telling him that the boys didn't seem to see her as a girl, or if they did, it was more as a sister than anything else. She never knew whether this was because the Headmaster's daughter was considered out of bounds or if her being at the top of the class scared them off.

The doctor held the conversation to recollections of their rival schools, and though Liza enjoyed reminiscing with him, she was still waiting hopefully for him to say something about a job. She didn't see how she could bring it up.

"I'll be going close to Willowbrook tomorrow," he said. "My parents live in Springbeck, a tiny place. Do you know it?"

"We used to hike there. It's lovely."

"Come along, if you're off duty," he said, as casually as if he were asking her to the canteen for coffee. "We can go hill walking."

Liza was speechless with surprise. While she tried to organize her thoughts, she heard the twelve slow solemn bells of midnight hammer Friday the thirteenth into the past. Before she could decide how to deal with this amazing invitation, Clare stepped out and called them.

"Dr. Peterson, you're wanted in Coronary Care."

His eyes met Liza's. Each knew the other's concern — was their old man in trouble? Liza wanted to go to the Unit with the doctor, but he hadn't asked her. She would have to wait.

She and Clare watched him stride toward the lifts. When he had gone,

Clare said, "In a way, I can see why you would go to the ends of the earth with that man."

Liza sighed deeply. "That's not what he's asking me to do. He just invited me to the Lake District for the weekend!"

"Liza, that's lovely: much better, in fact."

"To visit his parents," Liza added quickly. "But I'm not sure he meant it. He just asked me — out of the blue. What should I say?"

"You're off duty. Were you doing anything else?"

"You know I'm not."

Clare pursed her lips and thought. "A weekend in the Lake District is just what you need, But what about the job? What did he say?"

"Still not a word about it! Maybe he thinks he needs to know me better. That must be why he's invited me. If it's some extra-ordinary job in a far-away place, he'd want to know a lot about the person he takes along. I probably should accept his invitation."

"And it will be fun," Clare said. "Remember Cumbria in the spring. It's the Garden of Eden. I half envy you, Liza."

"Only I'm not sure what I should do about his invitation. It was so casual."

"Well, what did you say?"

"Nothing. You called him before I could answer. I can't bring up the subject very well. Suppose he doesn't ask again," Liza moaned.

"Then it would appear he didn't want you very badly."

Liza found little comfort in Clare's logic, but the arrival of a maternity case took her mind off her problems for the next half hour.

When she returned to the admissions office, Clare said, "Dr. Peterson was back. Our old man in Coronary Care is fine."

"Oh good!" Liza smiled. "He probably knows Dr. Peterson won't allow any relapse."

"There's something for you." Clare pointed to the back of her littered desk. Liza saw a folded sheet with her own name scrawled across it. She immediately recognized Doctor Peterson's masterful, but almost illegible handwriting.

She studied the short note a full minute before turning to Clare with a little giggle of delight. "He really does want me to go with him!"

Re-reading his note, which seemed completely out of character for him, she knew she must go with him. She couldn't ignore his cry for help.

He had written: "Without you, I'll fall asleep at the wheel, be deprived of a hiking companion, and disappoint my parents by failing, yet again, to bring home a nice girl."

He'd call at the Nurses' Residence soon after eight to see if she'd be kind enough to come along and prevent these calamities.

3

LIZA perched on the cold cement wall in front of the Nurses' Residence. Her lumpy duffel bag lay at her feet.

She'd fled from Casualty at the earliest decent moment after the day staff began arriving, and had rushed to the Coronary Care Unit to check on their cardiac arrest patient. He was awake and smiling and had raised a thumb in a feeble but triumphant gesture.

In the short time since then, she'd been making one quick decision after another — what to wear, what to take, should she try to borrow hiking boots or use her old worn-out pair? What could she take as a gift for her hostess?

Would it rain? Might there still be snow in the hills? Should she take her old crampons and ice axe, or would that look silly?

In the end, she'd panicked. Fearing the doctor would arrive before she was ready, she had impulsively thrown everything she liked best into the duffel bag. She put in, as a house gift, a box of lavender soap she'd splurged on but never opened.

She dressed in tan slacks and her warmest jumper, a forest green turtle neck. Her fly-away curls were crammed into a matching green woolly cap. A few shining tendrils had already corkscrewed out of captivity to halo her face. A brown anorak lay on the wall beside her.

Seeing Clare's old car coming from the car park, she stepped out to the curb and hailed her.

"So, you're going. You're lucky. It will be dreamy . . . "

"Don't sound so wistful," Liza chided. "You can still go home to Willowbrook every free weekend if you choose."

Clare laughed. "Meanwhile, who would sand my floors and peel my wallpaper and . . . "

"See," Liza interrupted, "You've let your nesting instinct spoil your fun. You can peel wallpaper when you're old and . . . "

Liza stopped abruptly, for she saw Dr. Peterson's little green Morgan speeding toward them. Her pulse raced as she reached for her bag. Then, she saw that he wasn't slowing as he approached. To her amazement, he sped past without even noticing her.

What was more shocking was that Martha Newman, looking happy and excited, chattered away beside him.

"Did I see what I thought I saw?" Clare demanded.

"I'm afraid so," Liza stated flatly. "I'll see you Monday, Clare." She turned to go back to the Residence.

"Oh, Liza dear, don't be so hasty. He's probably just running Martha home." Clare grasped her friend's hand.

Liza looked at her watch. "I'm not hasty. He wrote that he'd pick me up around eight. It's now eight twenty. I'm tired — of everything. I just want to sleep."

Clare watched her pick up her bag and walk doggedly toward the entrance. At the door a student nurse met her. They talked a moment, then walked down the steps together and the student went on.

Liza said, "He tried to call me, anyway. I'd already gone but he left a message, not that it makes much difference."

Clare waited.

"He's delayed — can't leave before ten thirty."

"Good, you can get a little sleep before you go," Clare said cheerfully.

"I'm not going. Martha can keep him awake. I suppose he thinks that if he can turn me on at the drop of a hat, he can turn me off to suit his whims, too. I never should have thought of going with him. I was out of my head."

Clare climbed out of her car and faced her friend, "Tell me, Liza, what do you want from Dr. Peterson — a chance at an interesting job or his exclusive attention? Was this some kind of ego trip, after all?"

"Clare, how would you feel?"

"When people do things impulsively, mix-ups can happen. I think you would realize that, if anyone but Martha had been with the doctor. And he did try to call you. He certainly wouldn't expect you to be sitting out here in the cold waiting, either."

Reluctantly, Liza admitted Clare was right. With a pang of shame, she saw herself as ridiculously eager.

"Right, I won't unpack," she conceded. "I'll lie down, and if he comes back for me, I might go, since I haven't anything very important to do — unless Martha's going. I'm sure he doesn't need us both."

Clare settled back behind the wheel. "Have a super weekend."

★ ★ ★

By eleven they were nearly out of London. The Morgan ate up the miles. They'd put down the top and the sun beat down on them from a cloudless sky. Liza's long curls streamed behind her like a bright banner.

In Windermere, they bought cheese and crackers and fruit for a picnic and climbed a knoll above the lake. Dr. Peterson reached down to help her up and then continued to walk hand in hand with her.

Liza found this pleasant but troubling. She didn't want to let her hand hang limp, but neither did she want to grasp his too ardently.

"Look, a yacht race," she exclaimed when they reached the viewpoint. "And what a perfect breeze!"

They watched the multicoloured spinnakers blossom across the blue lake as one yacht after another started the downwind leg of the race.

"Have you done any sailing?" Dr.

Peterson asked as they set about unpacking their lunch.

"Some. What about you?" Liza turned and found Dr. Peterson gazing at her in a way she found un-nerving.

"A long time ago," he said.

"Yes, me too — a long time ago."

She wanted to tell him about the heavenly summers spent on her grandmother's yacht, but thought better of it, not wanting to tell him how it had ended.

She still suffered an agony of guilt whenever she thought about the couple who had bought the yacht. They'd invited her to sail with them to the West Indies. She'd just begun her training and resisted the temptation to go.

A mayday call from somewhere west of the Canaries was the last anyone ever heard of the yacht or its owners.

Liza would go through life wondering if she might have made the difference. She knew the boat so well.

Dr. Peterson brought her back to the

present, saying, "It's too bad, but we'll need to be on our way soon. I didn't mean to start so late."

Liza expected he was about to either explain or apologize for keeping her waiting nearly three hours. He did neither.

I should have known he's not the sort to offer excuses, she thought.

At ten thirty when he'd finally turned up, he seemed to Liza unusually cheerful.

After helping her with her seatbelt, he told her he, too, had visited their cardiac arrest patient that morning. "It's gratifying," he said, "To see a man so happy to be alive."

Liza gazed at the resolute profile of the man who had literally forced his patient to live. She looked at his big brown hands grasping the wheel. I do want to work with him, she thought.

He turned and smiled at her, and they had set off as though everything were going according to plan, and Liza's awful moments of doubt and disappointment a few hours before had never happened.

Now, creeping out of Windermere behind a slow-moving caravan, he said, "I should warn you about my mother. She's trying to marry me off."

Liza was at a loss for an answer to that.

"Of course, she's too busy now to be a real menace," he went on. "Their practice doubles when the tourists begin to flock in."

"Your parents are doctors?" Liza realized how little she knew about him.

"My father is, though I'm trying to talk him into retiring in the autumn. My mother's a nurse."

"Mine is too. She was the school nurse at Willowbrook."

"And now?"

"She left to . . . re-marry."

From her tone, he gathered this wasn't a happy subject, he said, "And of course, your grandmother was a nurse. You must tell me about her."

She wanted to, but this was not to be the moment. They had reached Grasmere where he stopped to pick up a jar of heather honey for his mother.

"Are you sure she won't mind about me — just turning up?"

"I've phoned her. She's delighted. And so am I. You make this long trip fun, Liza."

She liked hearing him say her name, which he never had done before. "The pleasure is mine, Dr. Peterson," she murmured.

He frowned. "When you call me that, I feel like I'm on duty. Please call me Andrew."

Anxious to try it, she said, "Fine, Andrew. Dr. Peterson is just a man I knew in London."

They'd come into familiar countryside. Liza's eyes followed old stone walls that divided the world into patchwork pieces. New lambs already frolicked in the lower pastures, though snow had only recently melted on the peaks. Long narrow waterfalls, gleaming like zippers on the brown velvet hills, fed rivers that were flecked with frothy foam.

"It's so beautiful!" she shouted.

"Do you ever think of coming back here to live?"

"Maybe when I'm old. I really do love it."

"Then why wait until you're old?"

She leaned closer so she wouldn't have to shout. "You know why. I want to see new places now, not go back to old ones. But it's dreamy being here today."

I'd be missing all this, she thought, if it weren't for Clare's common sense. I'd be sitting home pouting. She resolved to stop being so emotional.

It was late afternoon before they reached Springbeck. Because the main road by-passed Willowbrook School, Andrew offered to make a detour so Liza could see her former home. She hesitated, torn between a desire to revisit the scene of her childhood and a reluctance to approach it as an outsider.

56

"No, thank you," she said at last.

The Peterson's house turned out to be one she had often noticed.

"I always admired this avenue of maples, and the plants in the bay window and the rock gardens," she exclaimed.

"My grandfather planted those maples," Andrew proudly informed her.

Built of the local green slate, the big house with its attached surgery stood on the outskirts of the village, facing the steep, dark hillsides that swoop down to Borrowdale Valley.

As soon as they were out of the car, Mrs. Peterson bustled down the front steps to greet them. She was a sweet, white-haired, round little woman, who darted about and chattered. She couldn't settle down until she had the kettle on and the tea cups out.

"Now, Andrew," she said, plumping down into a corner of the sofa, "Tell me all about Liza."

Smiling and unperturbed, he said,

"I'm sure she'll do that better than I can."

Liza was saved by the entrance, at that moment, of Dr. Andrew Peterson Senior. He was nice looking in a rugged, weather-beaten way, a tall, blue-eyed man with a great thatch of steel-grey hair. He was as placid and quiet as his wife was skittish and talkative.

Having finished a second cup of tea and a big piece of cream cake, Liza's attention wandered as the Petersons caught up on family news. She gazed lazily about the pleasant room. Everything had a mellowed look. The curtains and chintz-covered chairs were faded. The fine old Axminster carpets revealed where the main traffic flowed.

The sound of the Peterson's gentle voices lulled Liza into an overwhelming drowsiness. Mrs. Peterson caught her in the midst of a great, unconcealable yawn.

"Did this poor child work last night?" she demanded of Andrew; and not waiting for his answer, she said, "We'll talk at dinner. You two go straight up to bed."

"Why Mother! What are you saying!" he teased.

Mrs. Peterson blushed. "You rascal," she laughed. "Put Liza's bag in Virginia's room. Everything is ready."

As they were going up the stairs together, Liza asked, "Who is Virginia? Am I putting her out?"

"She's my sister, and she's already out — all the way out in St. John's, Newfoundland, unfortunately. Her husband is a registrar in Geriatrics there and hating every minute of it. That's why . . . "

He stopped short. When next he spoke it was to tell Liza, "The second door on the left, and there's a bathroom opposite."

He put her bag on a chair. "You'll be all right?"

She nodded and he left.

The room was a pretty, frilly, girl's room, but Liza's attention was immediately caught by the panorama beyond the wide window. She looked out on Derwent Water, lying unrippled in its deep valley. West of the lake rose Cat Bells, the range of blue hills she had climbed so often with the Willowbrook boys. The sun was already hovering above the long ridge. She opened her window and heard doves cooing in the pine tree in the garden.

It seemed she had just fallen asleep when she awoke from a dream of walking with her father.

She realized after a moment it had been Andrew's voice that had wakened her. He was tapping at her door.

"May I come in?" He came without waiting for an answer. "Did you sleep?" Again, he spoke before she could answer. "I want to give you a little warning of what's probably going to happen at dinner."

Liza was suddenly wide awake. "What do you mean?"

"My parents like you, as I knew they would. And I think you like them?"

Liza nodded, trying to hide her alarm. Had he been serious about his mother wanting to marry him off? But that's ridiculous, she decided.

"You know, I told you Virginia is away in Newfoundland. She's miserably homesick. Things haven't worked out well for them over there."

He paced the room. Liza had never seen him like this.

"Mother wants to fly out to be with her a while. Someone will be needed to take her place here. The nurse who used to come has moved away."

He stopped pacing and stood beside Liza's bed. "Mother will leave about the time your locum ends at St. Anne's. If you haven't already accepted a position, she'd like to speak to you about coming here."

Liza's heart sank. So this was the job! He didn't want a helpmate in his African adventures. He wanted a housekeeper for his father!

And this was the real reason he wanted her to come with him: he hadn't cared about her company or any of the nice things he'd written in his note. That was just a lure.

She wanted to turn her face to the wall and not have to cope with him, not have to think about a way to refuse politely.

He sat on the edge of her bed. "I don't want you to feel pressured because of . . . "

"Because of being a guest?"

"I've made an awkward muddle of this, Liza. I was going to offer you the job when Mother called a few days ago to ask if I might know someone. I knew you would need something soon.

"But last night when we talked you were so definite about wanting to travel. I was pretty sure you wouldn't want to consider this. It seemed silly to even speak to you about it. I was going to look for someone else."

"Then why did you ask me to come?" Her voice wavered, and she hoped he wouldn't notice. She felt at a

62

disadvantage, lying on her back looking up at him.

He kept her waiting for his answer, his dark eyes brooding as he gazed down at her.

"I'd made some complicated arrangements and . . . " He looked away.

She thought that was all the answer she would get, but after a long pause, he turned back to her and said, "I asked you to come because I wanted to, Liza. That's all."

She smiled and impulsively grasped his hand a moment. "That's nice," she murmured.

"And why were you willing to come?" he asked.

She wished her motives were as simple, that she could say: just because I wanted to.

She clasped the covers about her and propped herself against the padded headboard. Her copper curls were like a sunburst against the white satin. Andrew's gaze was becoming embarrassing. She fidgeted with the sheet, took a deep breath and, avoiding his eyes, began.

"Clare — Sister Robson — told me you'd been asking when my locum would end. I thought you might want me to work with you . . . somewhere. I thought perhaps you had invited me here because you wanted to become better acquainted before offering me a job, that is, a job with you, away somewhere."

"You were right about one thing. I do want to become better acquainted."

It flashed through her mind that if this were so, why was last night the first time he'd ever really chatted with her at St. Anne's. He'd never even joined her for a cup of coffee in the canteen. He always chose to sit with Martha.

He went on. "And we might work together. If you took Mother's job it would last only a month, and of course, my job at St. Anne's is temporary. I've been mulling over a lot of possibilities."

Was he giving her reason to hope? She didn't know what to think.

"We'll talk tomorrow," he said. "We have to go down to dinner now."

He rose to leave. "I didn't want mother to spring this on you tonight without warning you first. I've told her I didn't think you wanted to work in Springbeck, after all, but now that you're here she insists you must have a chance to decide for yourself."

Liza's mind was in turmoil as she quickly dressed in her all-purpose blue plaid shirt-dress.

She glanced out the window at the sunset's last red glow. A late rook flapped across the shadowy scene. It's so familiar and dear, she thought — this lovely Cumbria. She felt a little shudder and fancied the winds of the past and future mingled in the sudden breeze wafting through her window.

Hurrying downstairs, she found Andrew and his father in front of the fire in the living room.

"The choice is whisky or whisky, I'm afraid," said Dr. Peterson, uncorking a bottle of malt.

Mrs. Peterson joined them for drinks, but soon excused herself to finish preparing the meal.

"May I help?" Liza offered.

"Thank you, but I'm too disorganized to be helped."

Liza felt uneasy at first about the prospect of having to deal with Mrs. Peterson's job offer. But by the time Andrew had poured her a second glass of the excellent Burgundy that accompanied the venison, she had forgotten everything but present pleasure.

To Liza's surprise and relief, the subject of working in Springbeck never did arise.

At ten Dr. Peterson was called to the cottage hospital. Andrew went with him. Now, Liza thought, Mrs. Peterson will ask me while we're alone. She was mistaken.

"Why don't you go ahead up," Mrs. Peterson suggested. "Andrew will be thumping your door bright and early tomorrow if the weather is good. The dishwasher will make short work of this pile."

Feeling she really meant it, Liza said goodnight as soon as they had cleared the table. As she climbed the stairs, still uncommitted, she wondered if Mrs. Peterson had decided she didn't want her.

★ ★ ★

As Mrs. Peterson had warned, there was no lying in on Sunday. Andrew started knocking and calling at seven thirty.

"You're pretty in the morning," he exclaimed. "I thought girls weren't supposed to be."

An hour later they stepped out into a perfect April morning. Andrew spread an Ordinance Survey map on the long bonnet of the Morgan and they planned their day's hike — to Watendlath, over the fell to Rosthwaite, across the river at Grange, up Cat Bells and home.

Andrew slid the map into his pack

with their rain gear and lunch, and they set off along the avenue of maples.

"It must have been your great grandfather who planted these maples. They've been here a long, long time," Liza observed.

"So was my grandfather," Andrew laughed. "He had this practice forty years. My father has had it thirty five. If I took it, we could make it a century of Petersons."

"But you wouldn't take it." Liza had not tried to hide the alarm she felt, and Andrew looked at her, surprised.

"One could do worse."

"But it would be such a ... " She had almost said a waste of your abilities, but saw in time how insulting that would be to his father — and his grandfather.

"It would be such a quiet life, after the things you have done and ... "

"A quiet life begins to look good after five years with a roving medical mission."

Oh please, don't talk like that Liza

thought. She said, "Those years must have been so rewarding and exciting."

Steering her from the pavement onto a grassy track, he said, "They were varied. I'll admit that."

"And all the places you must have seen!"

"None more beautiful than what we're looking at now."

"Yes, you know that because you've seen the other places."

He helped her over a stile and led her into a mossy wood where they followed a narrow footpath. "I can spare you a lot of miles if you'll take my word for it."

"Thanks, but I want to find out for myself. I don't want to be spared those miles," Liza declared.

"I know." His tone was bleak.

"You think I'm silly?"

"Not silly, no. I do understand."

They walked in silence a while, Liza a few steps behind him on the path. He stopped and turned so suddenly she walked into his arms. He looked down into her green eyes a long moment, holding her with his gaze.

At last he said, "There's a place you should see. I'll take you there today. I don't take just anyone there; you'll see, it's special."

He seemed to Liza to be half serious and half joking, and in the same tone she said, "I have a secret grove here, too. I found it when I fell way behind on a school hike. If we're near it today and you treat me very well, I might show it to you."

He took her arm and they walked side by side, slowly and sometimes awkwardly on the narrow path, strolling, not hiking, Liza thought, but it was pleasant.

"I used to pester my parents to come and have a picnic in my lovely spot," she said. "They never said no, but we didn't do it either. Father wasn't very athletic."

"And now where are your parents? In London?"

"No, my father died last year. Just

now my mother is trying to sell my grandmother's place in Scotland. She lived in a crumbly old castle on the Isle of Mull."

She chattered on to avoid his saying he was sorry about her father. She never knew how to answer that.

"I stayed with Gran every summer while I was growing up. I admired her more than anyone."

"And she inspired you to become a nurse?"

"Yes, when she was my age, she was already working in Asia. You know about her starting the mission.

"Then when the war started, she came home to work in hospitals near Portsmouth.

"After the war she went to Australia on one of the last grain clippers and married the Captain. She was thirty then and he was much older. My mother was their only child."

With an embarrassed little laugh, she said, "I'm sorry, you didn't ask for a three-generation saga."

"But what an amazing woman! And your mother was a nurse, too. Did she work in Assam?"

"No, she was married right after her training. I shouldn't criticize: I might not be here if she hadn't. But I intend to avoid entangling alliances until I'm thirty like my Grandmother."

There, she thought. I've put that on record.

Andrew held her hand as she teetered along the edge of a boggy patch.

He asked, "What will you do if, to coin a phrase, you fall in love."

She laughed. "I haven't had that problem yet, have you?"

She was embarrassed when she realized he was giving her question serious thought. She shouldn't have asked. Somehow, his question wasn't personal, but hers was. She wished she could take it back.

"I thought once that I was," he said. "But in retrospect — no."

While she was considering this complicated piece of information, he went on: "There are different kinds of love between men and women."

Impulsively, she contradicted him. "No, love is love is love."

He smiled, and she thought there was a bit of condescension in the way he looked at her. "I expect you have a lot to learn about love."

This was too patronizing! "How do you know so much about it if . . . " Her wiser self prevailed, though a little late, and she dropped the subject. After a few minutes she said, "Your mother hasn't spoken to me about the job."

"She knows I've just mentioned it to you. She probably wants to give you time to think about it. I expect she'll speak to you tonight. Have you made up your mind?"

"A dozen times — different every time."

"Then I mustn't talk about it. I promised Mother I wouldn't try to persuade you."

"If you were to try, would it be to take it or not to take it?"

He shook her in mock anger. "You crafty imp! That's not fair. I won't answer."

"But it's part of the data I need for making my decision," she argued.

"It shouldn't be."

At noon, as Andrew led her toward the stepping stones across the river, Liza declared she was starving.

"Let's have our picnic by the water. It makes such pretty music, and I'll perish if we don't eat soon," she said.

"If you could hold out a little further, we can eat in the special place I told you about."

Liza looked across the river to the forest below Castle Crag. "Andrew!" she gasped. "Your place is my place!"

"What are you talking about?"

"I know where you're taking us."

"I doubt that. You'd never find this place."

Liza was convinced he'd never find her hiding place, and yet, as they moved ever faster in silent suspense toward the base of the crag, each realized they were heading for the same spot.

The natural enclosure, hidden in the dense little forest, was roofed by the tangled branches of an ancient rowan tree. Except for a narrow pass between two boulders, it was walled by the curving cliff face and huge rocks that had broken away from it.

A waterfall trickled off the cliff. Every rock was upholstered in deep moss. Gorse blossomed beside the entrance and clumps of long pointed leaves indicated foxgloves would send up their vivid spikes to adorn the walls in summer.

They stood inside, completely concealed.

"It's just as I remember," Liza breathed."

Andrew put down his pack and looked across at her.

She was flushed from the little scramble to the entrance. Her eyes were shining with pleasure as she sighed, "Oh, Andrew! Isn't it heavenly?"

"Yes, heavenly, and there's even an angel here this time," he murmured.

"A starving angel," she laughed, lunging for the pack which he'd placed on a handy table rock.

"Wait!"

She straightened, finding herself very close to him.

"I'm hungry, too." He leaned forward, his arms at his sides, and buried his face in her curls. "Liza, Liza," he whispered.

She stood as though mesmerized while he raised her hands and kissed her finger-tips. Then he caught her in a sudden embrace. His lips moved across her face and settled gently upon hers.

Liza stiffened, resisting him, but soon surrendered. Her eyes closed, and it seemed that in his arms she became weightless. At last, he held her at arm's length and again whispered her name, as though savouring it.

So, this is the trap, Liza thought, this melting and merging with someone dear. It's remarkably wonderful. I almost forgot it's not for me.

She drew a deep tremulous breath. "Andrew, I've just told you, I don't want romantic entanglements. Why are you doing this?"

He held her head against his chest and gently stroked her cheek as he considered her question. "Because I want to," he answered finally.

"That's often your reason for doing things, isn't it?"

"Can you think of a better one?"

"Not now." She couldn't think at all. She listened to the secret sounds of his heartbeats and his breathing. This calmed her racing pulse.

When, at last they turned their attention to lunch, Andrew said, "For one who plans to avoid entanglements, you're living pretty recklessly."

She had no answer to this.

Before leaving their secret glade, Andrew knelt at the base of the little waterfall and chose a sparkling piece of quartz from among the wet pebbles. He slipped it into his pocket.

"What's that for?" Liza asked.

He smiled and put an arm around her. "For remembering until we come back."

"Shall we come back?" she asked.

"Do you want to?"

"Oh yes!" she whispered.

"Then, I promise we shall."

4

I'M fevered with happiness, Liza thought, striding beside Andrew.

A soft rain had begun to fall as they left their corner of the forest. She raised her face, flushed from the excitement of his caresses, to the soothing coolness of raindrops. From the ridge of Cat Bells, she looked down at the lake on her right and the idyllic valley on her left and felt like the queen of the world surveying her kingdom.

They were off the ridge, slogging through wet bracken in companionable silence when they startled a shepherd who stepped through a gate in front of them. He recognized Andrew, and they talked briefly about the lamb crop and the weather. Andrew introduced Liza.

"Yes," the shepherd said, shaking her hand warmly. "We met when you were here before. You two were caught in the rain that day, too."

He had been smiling until he saw Andrew's strained look and realized he had made a mistake. Embarrassed, he mumbled, "Nice to see you." He doffed his cap and went on.

Andrew offered no explanation.

Liza's initial shock gave way to sympathy for the shepherd. He'd been so disconcerted, poor man. He didn't know that the other women in Andrew's life could be no concern of hers.

She wondered if it was Martha who had walked here with him. She mustn't care. But the thought of him with someone else in their special place hurt terribly.

She felt a tear merge with the rain running down her cheek and angrily wiped it away. The walk wasn't fun any more, and now one boot was hurting her foot.

They came to the road. A Land Rover stopped.

"Hi, Andy! Want a lift?" The driver was a pretty girl; another sat beside her.

Andrew greeted them as old friends. He introduced Liza who rode in silence while the three gossiped about mutual acquaintances.

Of course, a man like Andrew would have a string of women, Liza thought. Look how he swept me off my feet. Why should I think I'm more important to him than scores of others.

I can't complain, though. I don't want him or any other man — for at least another eight years. Still . . . Oh dear, I have been foolish.

Andrew was insisting they be dropped at the end of his street, saying, "There's no need to go out of your way. The rain has stopped."

"Next time don't stay away so long," the driver called.

The breeze was shaking water from the fat maple buds, so they walked in the street to avoid the worst of it. Andrew said, "Liza, you're limping. What is it?"

"No, I'm all right."

She tried in vain to stop favouring

her left foot. Her old boots had held up well enough while they were dry, but once they'd become water-logged, they had begun to disintegrate.

She feared the left one was wearing a nasty blister on the side of her foot, but she didn't want Andrew to know. She didn't want him to touch her.

He did, though. As soon as they were in the house he had her boot off and scolded her for not telling him sooner she was having trouble. He went into the surgery for a dressing, and Liza heard him talking to his mother. They came back together and made a great fuss about her blister.

"Go have a nice hot bath," Mrs. Peterson ordered.

"Then let Andrew bandage your foot, and we'll have a cup of tea. He tells me you had a beautiful walk."

She came out of her bath refreshed, pink and glowing and smelling sweet from a dusting of powder.

Andrew waylaid her in the hall and went into her room with her to dress her blister. Though she tried to think of him as just a doctor treating a sore foot, the touch of his hands sent shivers up her spine.

When he finished, he smiled and said, "Please make an appointment for a return visit. Meanwhile leave your shoes off. Do you have slippers? Put them on and come for tea."

While Mrs. Peterson divided the left-over cream cake into quarters, Andrew went to call his father from the surgery.

"Did he have a patient?" Liza asked, knowing there would be no surgery hours on Sunday.

"No, this is our day to catch up on the paper-work," Mrs. Peterson sighed. "It's endless — more every year, it seems. It's high time we gave it all up, but I don't know what I'll do without it, either."

To Liza, it seemed cruel that the Petersons had spent the beautiful spring Sunday working inside. She wondered that anyone was willing to do single-handed general practice; it was so demanding.

The doctor looked weary when he joined them, but tea and the wonderfully wicked cream cake restored everyone's spirits. Liza felt a glimmer of the contentment and well-being she'd enjoyed the evening before.

Leaving out certain details, Andrew gave such an amusing account of their walk that she felt happy about it again, herself. It really had been glorious.

She looked at the handsome young doctor seated opposite her, and thought, how silly I am to be upset about his other women friends. He's exactly right for me just now — good company, some completely meaningless but enjoyable romancing, and no threat at all to my goals.

When Mrs. Peterson rose to clear away the tea things, Liza said, "You must let me be useful now. I've done nothing to help."

"No, there's so little to do," said Mrs. Peterson.

But Liza was adamant. "Surely I can

help with dinner."

"Maybe you'd make the salad, then," the older woman conceded; but as they entered the kitchen, she said, "You can't walk around in those little slippers. Your poor feet will freeze."

Though Liza insisted her flip-flops were fine, Mrs. Peterson led her upstairs to her bedroom.

"I have a new pair of moccasins that Virginia sent from Canada — fleece lined, just the thing. And I think we wear about the same size."

While she rummaged about deep inside her walk-in closet, chattering incomprehensibly among the hems of dresses and coats, Liza looked around the pretty lilac and green bedroom.

The light glinted off a silver frame on the dressing table. Liza went closer and saw a photograph of Andrew and a smiling girl who looked a little like him. She had the same dark hair and the eager, vivacious look that Liza found so appealing in the rest of the family.

Mrs. Peterson backed out of her

closet, holding up the slippers and smiling with satisfaction. "I was sure they were in there."

She saw Liza looking at the photograph.

"Is that Virginia?"

Her smile vanished. She glanced out her open door and said in a low voice, "That's Flora, you know."

Sensing that Liza didn't know, she said, "Has Andrew not told you about Flora?"

Mrs. Peterson seemed so distraught, Liza wished she had not mentioned the girl. "No, he hasn't." She put on the slippers. "They're perfect," she announced.

Mrs. Peterson nodded absently. She was still gazing at the picture and said, "I keep this in here. Andrew had put it away. He can't look at it. I don't feel that way. We all loved Flora."

Though Liza's curiosity was greatly aroused, she didn't ask who Flora was, for she seemed to be associated with some terrible unhappiness. The two women started out of the room, but Mrs. Peterson laid her hand on Liza's arm, detaining her.

"Perhaps I should tell you, just so you won't say anything that could upset Andrew." She closed the door.

"I'm not surprised he hasn't spoken about it." She led Liza to the picture. "Andrew and Flora became engaged when he was home on leave two years ago. When he returned to Africa, she begged to go with him. She was killed in the troubles there just a month later."

Liza gasped, and Mrs. Peterson paused so long it seemed she would say no more. Finally, she went on, but with obvious difficulty.

"Andrew has felt all this time that it was his fault, because he allowed her to go to a place he knew could be very dangerous. We've had to be so careful what we say. In spite of the cheerful front he puts on, he's far from being over his grief."

"That's why it made us so happy

that he brought you home with him. Perhaps he sees, at last, that he has to get on with his life."

Liza was too stunned by this revelation to be able to think straight. She said, simply, "How sad for all of you. I'm sorry."

Mrs. Peterson shrugged resignedly, straightened the picture a fraction of an inch and wordlessly led Liza back downstairs.

What she'd just learned about Andrew had aroused her deepest sympathy. It also explained why, from the day she'd met him, he had discouraged her from working in the Third World.

I can probably forget about his ever taking me there to work with him, she decided.

She found him still engrossed in conversation with his father. Dr. Peterson rose stiffly from his chair, and Liza heard him tell his wife, "We'll be in my office. Andrew has an interesting idea . . . "

Liza went to work on the salad

while Mrs. Peterson concentrated on a Hollandaise sauce for the broccoli. She was unusually quiet, leaving Liza to re-arrange the pieces of the puzzle called Andrew Peterson.

She supposed the shepherd had mistaken her for Flora. Poor Andrew! No wonder he had looked so stricken and had made no explanation.

And if he had taken Flora to their forest hideaway, how could she begrudge them that? She recalled his saying, "I don't take just anyone there." Her image of him as a Don Juan had been unfair.

She thought of the guilt she'd felt about the couple that perished on her grandmother's yacht. What torment Andrew must suffer — blaming himself for his fiancée's death.

Her grim reverie was interrupted by the fierce rattling of the double boiler.

"This is when the sauce tries to curdle," Mrs. Peterson warned.

As soon as this crisis stage was past she began describing the minutiae of making successful sauces. Liza tried to appear interested, but her attention soon flagged.

"Of course, the simplest kind of cooking satisfies my husband; and that reminds me, Andrew has told you I'm going to be with Virginia in June?"

Liza was suddenly alert. "Yes, he did, and you need someone . . . "

"Yes, we've tried to persuade Virginia to come home for a holiday, but she won't come without her husband, and he can't leave. I simply must go to them, so we do need someone here to help."

She gave the sauce a final stir, set it aside and continued.

"The few times I've had to be away, we've hired a practice nurse who lived in — for the telephone, you know. She did some cooking, too. She can't come this time. Andrew tells me he's asked you if you'd like to come."

Liza had to raise her voice above the whir of the electric blender. "Yes, he did speak of it."

"There's no need for you to decide quickly, but if you would like to know more about what's involved the dates, duties, salary, that sort of thing . . . "

"I have decided," Liza heard herself saying. "I think I would like to come."

Mrs. Peterson turned off the blender and gave Liza her full attention. "Don't rush into this, my dear. Andrew said he thought you preferred working abroad."

"I can do that later."

"I'm so pleased! If you're sure about this, we can discuss details after dinner."

"I'm quite sure," Liza answered, with more conviction than she felt.

Mrs. Peterson hugged her. "Wonderful, wonderful! Don't tell the men. Let me surprise them. They'll both be so delighted."

At dinner she raised her glass and announced, "We'll drink to Liza tonight. She's agreed to hold the fort for me while I'm with Virginia."

Both men beamed at her. Old Dr.

Peterson, that man of few words, said, "Liza, I can't tell you how pleased I am. We'll have a good time here."

"Not too good, mind!" his wife admonished, "or I'll see that you get an ogre next time, instead of a pretty young girl."

Liza, herself, was still in shock over what she had done. She had accepted the job purely on impulse. She remembered a quotation from somebody — 'The heart has its reasons which reason knows nothing of'. It's the only explanation for what I've done.

Andrew was watching her over his glass. He smiled, but said nothing.

★ ★ ★

Their weekend together finished at four on the bleakest of Monday afternoons.

Liza felt Andrew gently shaking her. Coming up from deep slumber, she awoke to a crick in her neck, and the car's door handle pressing painfully against her side.

She closed her eyes again, wishing she could let the hum of the engine and the metronomic click of the wipers lull her back to sleep.

She felt the little car turn into the narrow street beside the Nurses' Residence. Andrew's big warm hand grasped both of hers.

She looked at him for the first time in hours, and found him as devastating to her peace of mind as when she'd closed her eyes somewhere south of Penrith.

As he backed into a parking space, Liza wondered how she ought to respond if he were inclined to kiss her goodbye.

The night before she had listened for his footsteps on the stairs, half hoping he'd come in to kiss her goodnight.

He had remained downstairs talking with his parents, and she had finally fallen asleep with her bedside lamp still burning.

Since then, everything had changed. They had not actually quarrelled, but each had said things that upset the other.

He helped her out of the car and was about to carry her bag up the steps, but she said, "Oh, goodness, I can take that myself."

"Well, see you on duty, then." He looked at his watch. "In just five hours. Thank you, Liza, for coming with me, and for . . ."

She didn't linger. "Thank you for a nice weekend," she called from the top of the steps.

★ ★ ★

Her nap in the car, not enough to prepare her for the night's work ahead, made it difficult to fall asleep again.

London's noisy late afternoon traffic clogged the little street outside her window. And now, images of the weekend crowded her mind. *If only I could remember Sunday morning forever and never again think of today.*

The day had started well enough with a big breakfast in the Peterson kitchen. She and Andrew hadn't left 'til ten, after he'd sat in on his father's morning surgery.

While the men were busy, Liza and Mrs. Peterson discussed what Mrs. Peterson laughingly called 'the transfer of power' in June.

The prospect of spending a month in Springbeck had become fairly attractive to Liza. At that point, she still clung to the faint hope of overseas work with Andrew afterward.

"Your parents are wonderful," she said as they waved to them and set off in the rain.

The trouble began a half hour out of Springbeck when Liza said, "I forgot my boots and slacks. I'm so sorry. They were still wet, so I didn't pack them. They're in the back hall."

"No problem," Andrew assured her. "I'll have to come back soon. I'll be called for an interview."

Seeing Liza's puzzled frown, he

said, "I'm going to apply for Dad's practice."

"But Andrew, you can't."

"You're wrong, my dear Liza. I can. I took a GP traineeship before I decided to do surgery."

"But it doesn't seem very logical," she said with too much vehemence.

Now, lying in her room, she remembered exactly how he looked at her with that calm, resolute expression. She supposed he was unaware that he had just smashed completely her beautiful dream of working abroad with him.

He seemed surprised at her lack of enthusiasm. "So you don't think Springbeck deserves me?" he quipped.

"But why . . . ?"

"I've been thinking about this for quite a while," he explained. "Last night I finally decided."

She remembered that when she woke in the night to turn off her lamp, he and his father were still talking downstairs. "Is it just because you like

Cumbria so much?"

"That's only one of several reasons. Another is that Dad can't go through even one more winter alone. He's having a lot of trouble with arthritis."

"But that doesn't mean you have to take his practice?"

Andrew looked at her with a trace of annoyance. "You certainly don't think much of my decision, do you?"

"I'm just surprised." Trying for a less critical tone, she smiled and said, "I know. You just want to make a century of Petersons."

He laughed. "I had forgotten that reason."

Liza felt she must accept her disappointment and, if she couldn't say anything good about Andrew's idea, say nothing at all.

He looked tired this morning. The scar across his forehead appeared more vivid. Liza recalled that he was, after all, a man who had suffered a great deal — the loss of Flora, the injuries he himself had sustained in Africa.

She couldn't blame him for choosing Cumbria now.

At last she said, "Well, if that's what you want, I wish you luck." She meant it to sound more encouraging than it did.

They rounded a curve and found the road full of sheep. The shepherd glanced back at them but could do nothing to let them by. Andrew stopped the car and they watched three collies herd the wet and bedraggled flock into a field farther along.

Before starting the car again, Andrew leaned across and kissed Liza. Her surprise was evident. "I just wanted to," he explained. She laughed.

A little later he said, "I'll tell you why I want to take my father's practice. When I talked to him about retiring, I soon realized he'd be miserable with nothing to do; so would my mother. They can't retire completely, but neither can they go on as they are."

"He should take a partner," Liza

exclaimed, certain that she'd hit upon the perfect solution. "The Health Service encourages partnerships and groups. I have a friend who . . . "

Andrew interrupted. "Unfortunately Dad's practice isn't big enough, except in summer when the tourists come. Anyway, there's only the one house."

"I don't see how your having the practice will help them . . . "

"If I had it, Dad could do locums for me and Mother could still work in the practice part time. They could stay in their home. I don't need that big house."

Though her better judgement told her to drop the subject, Liza persisted. "But what about you? What about your surgical training. It would be wasted!" The moment the words were out, she regretted them.

He didn't try to hide his irritation. "Am I wasting it now, caring for people in London who are hurt or ill? Are only people in what you consider interesting places worth treating?"

"You know I don't mean that."

"No, I'm not sure you don't mean precisely that."

"You have to admit you've trained to do more than general practice."

"Yes, and I can give my patients the benefit of that training wherever I am."

"But you specialized. You won't do any surgery in Springbeck. All that skill . . . "

She realized how stridently she was arguing. "I'm sorry, Andrew. I didn't mean to tell you what you should do. Forgive me."

He had smiled then, but it was a tense smile, not a happy one. He said, "You care. Don't apologize for that."

They turned onto the motorway soon after, and riding in silence, Liza tried to orient herself in their relationship. What did Andrew want from her?

She said, "Yesterday you wouldn't tell me whether you wanted me to take your mother's job, remember?"

"That's right. It was important for

you to decide for yourself, without persuasion."

"Will you tell me now, honestly, are you glad I took it?"

"I'm delighted."

"So you did want me to take it?"

"I hoped you would."

"But you wouldn't do anything to influence me?"

"Liza, what are you getting at? Why don't you have a little rest while you can. Come, put your head on my shoulder."

"Good idea," she agreed, but she didn't accept the offer of his shoulder. Instead, she hunched down in her seat and closed her eyes.

She wanted to put some emotional distance between them, and lying on his shoulder was not the way to start.

Now, tossing and turning in her bed with further sleep eluding her, she recalled Andrew's answer when she had asked if he'd ever been in love — "In retrospect, no."

This, in the light of what she

had learned about his fiancée, was a horrendous admission. Poor Flora!

She threw off a blanket, plumped up her pillow, and vowed she would put Dr. Andrew Peterson out of her mind.

5

LIZA was already busy scrubbing down and resetting a trolley when Clare arrived in Casualty.

"Liza Carter! I can't stand the shock. You're here fifteen minutes early."

"I couldn't sleep," Liza explained in a dreary voice, hardly looking up from her work.

She'd thought a leisurely meal would perk up her spirits, but the nearly empty dining room seemed oppressive. She had to face it — she'd hoped Andrew might be there.

When she'd finished eating, there was still time to kill before going on duty. She went up to the Coronary Care Unit to see how their old man was doing.

"Ah, you must be looking for Amos Harper," said the Sister. "He's been moved out to ward six."

She peeked into the four-bed ward and found him chatting with an elderly woman visitor.

Since the only refuge left was work, she had relieved Nurse Wright ahead of time.

As Clare headed toward the office to take the day report, she said, "I know why you're here early, you couldn't wait to tell me about Dr. Peterson's job offer."

"That wasn't what I had hoped," Liza answered glumly.

"Cheer up. I have a great idea for you. We must talk later." She hurried on.

When they went for their break, which turned out to be the first chance they had to talk, Nurse Daniels joined them.

Waiting for the thin stream of coffee to dribble from the throbbing machinery, Liza wondered about Clare's great idea for her. Her ideas always involved staying in London.

She saw Andrew sitting at the end

of the crowded room. As usual, Martha was with him, doing most of the talking. He didn't notice Liza. All night they'd exchanged only a few words, rather formally, she thought, everything considered.

Nurse Daniels and Clare were discussing him and Martha in hushed tones.

"It's to do with her Community Medicine project," Nurse Daniels was saying.

Clare told Liza, "Martha's been to Paris this weekend."

"She couldn't be. We saw her . . . " Liza didn't want to say it — "Riding with Dr. Peterson."

Nurse Daniels, sounding happy about Martha's good fortune, said, "Yes, it was the doctor who arranged everything for her, all very suddenly, she told me he even drove her to the airport Saturday morning because she overslept."

"So that was it." Liza muttered.

Nurse Daniels continued. "She'll be working with a friend of the doctor's for three weeks next term. She's over the moon."

"Hmm, Paris," Liza murmured. "How about that, Clare. Dr. Peterson found Martha a job in Paris."

At last the penny dropped. "The phone call he took at my desk! Oh, Liza! I gave you a false lead. But then I wonder why . . . "

Liza wondered too, why had he hung up the phone and asked for her? Why did he want to know when her locum ended. A call from Paris could have no connection with her.

They heard Dr. Peterson's bleep sounding. He left the canteen without looking right or left, followed closely by Martha.

Nurse Daniels said, "Such a nice girl, that poor Martha Newman."

"What do you mean — poor?" Liza asked.

"You wouldn't know, of course. It happened long before your time. She's an orphan. Her father was a surgeon here, a wonderful man. He and his wife were killed in a terrible road accident."

"Martha's older sister was hurt, too. She recovered, but I heard she was killed in another tragedy a few years later. Makes you wonder, doesn't it?"

Though minutes before Liza had looked enviously at Martha, she now felt a profound sympathy for her. She knew well enough the pain of losing a parent. What must it be to lose them both, and a sister, too!

She heard her page and rose to leave. Clare and Nurse Daniels looked at the clock and went with her.

Out in the corridor Liza saw Andrew at the far end, still listening to Martha, as though he could hardly tear himself from her.

An idea occurred to her. "Nurse Daniels, when did Martha lose her parents?"

The old nurse had to think. "It must be six or seven years ago."

"When Dr. Peterson was a registrar here?"

"Oh, I don't remember details like that. It seems so long ago now. Ask Dr. Peterson, why don't you?"

Liza wouldn't think of asking him, but she was quite sure he'd been at St. Anne's six years ago, just before he went to Africa.

Maybe he and Martha's father had been colleagues. Maybe that explained the special interest he took in her welfare.

"I almost forgot," Clare said. "I've heard of just the thing for you, Liza, at the Liverpool School of Tropical Medicine. Oh darn! I'll have to tell you later." She dashed off to answer her phone.

As she left, an ambulance arrived. Liza saw that the patient being wheeled in lay very still. Bright red blood smeared his shirt and darkened the grey blankets.

Andrew came striding from the doctor's room. After the briefest glance at the patient, he began giving orders.

"Oesophageal varices, Nurse Carter.

He's lost a lot of blood already. Get a sample to the lab for typing. We'll give him O Negative immediately, since he's in shock."

An hour passed, and for all their efforts, their patient's condition steadily deteriorated. The doctor was perspiring freely. He seemed to Liza to be unusually tense, and she wondered if he was feeling the effects of talking half the previous night with his father and then driving most of the day.

She herself was running on nervous energy. Intent though she was on carrying out his orders, Andrew's physical proximity was distracting. The hot little room, the frightened patient, the urgency to get him out of shock and to stop his internal bleeding all combined to build an almost palpable pressure.

At last the bleeding ceased. By five in the morning the patient was out of immediate danger.

"Come on, Liza, a cup of coffee will help." Andrew took her arm and headed for the canteen. She was speechless. Had she finally won the right to sit with him in public?

Of course, there was no public. They had the place to themselves. At this hour he ran no risk of Martha seeing them together.

Sitting there, exhausted, her mind bearly ticking over, Liza suddenly saw, clearly, what Andrew wanted of her — a spare, a substitute. Someone for when Martha had to go to Paris, or when Martha was asleep and he wanted company for coffee, a spare for his father's practice when his mother had to be away.

It wasn't a role she wanted. She couldn't endure another moment of it. She rose and left the canteen. At the door she glanced back at Andrew sitting alone, a rare sight. He looked puzzled.

Just a few more hours, she thought, and I can escape the futility of everything in sleep.

Clare caught up with her as she

was leaving in the morning. "I wanted to tell you this, Liza. It might be important for you to do something about it quickly."

"Ah, yes. The Liverpool School of Tropical Medicine. But I don't want to go to school. I want to go to work, preferably not in Liverpool."

"But this course is just made for you, Liza. My cousin is on the faculty and he's recruiting qualified people for a course on Third World Health Care."

Encouraged by Liza's slight show of interest, she went on eagerly, "I don't want you to leave London, but this sounds so right for you. You ought to apply."

"All right, Thanks, Clare. Do you have the address?"

Clare handed her not only the address, but the course prospectus, as well. "I asked him to send along the bumph for you. He hopes he'll hear from you."

As they stepped out into the bright morning, Clare was delighted to find her fiancé waiting for her.

Simon Crawford, a good looking, heavy-set man with eyes as green as Liza's, embraced Clare and planted a kiss in Liza's curls.

"I hear the lovely Liza's been to Cumbria. Tell me everything," he demanded. "Are you heading for darkest Africa with the handsome Dr. Peterson?"

As briefly as possible, she told him and Clare about Andrew's plan to work in Cumbria and about Mrs. Peterson's job offer.

"I promised her I'd spend June in Springbeck, but now I know it won't lead to anything else."

"You never know," Clare grinned. "But anyway, you ought to write to my cousin in Liverpool."

Liza did mean to write to him, but she didn't get around to it. Casualty was exceptionally busy, and she felt tired all the time. She diagnosed this as spring fever.

Most evenings she went to work early

enough to chat a while with Amos Harper. She felt drawn to the old man whom Andrew had pulled back into the land of the living. Except for his landlady, who came once to bring things from his room, he had no visitors, and he was a gregarious old man.

When he learned Liza had sailed the west coast of Scotland, he managed to turn most conversations to the subject of boats.

They knew many of the same lovely anchorages and had even competed in some of the same races. He proudly showed her photos of his precious old sloop, SONGSTRESS.

Liza enjoyed this reminiscing almost as much as Amos did. The present wasn't affording either of them much pleasure.

Several times Liza found Andrew visiting Amos. The old man idolized him. "A prince," he called him.

For some reason, Andrew was less cool and formal with Liza when they met in Andrew's room. The rest of the time he was like a stranger.

One evening, walking into Amos's ward, she was surprised to find the old man entertaining a visitor whom he introduced with a gleam of pride and pleasure in his eye.

"Nurse Carter, meet my son, Bobby."

A thin, sandy-haired, slightly ravaged-looking young man stood and extended his hand.

Amos said, "He's a drummer, a bit daft, but a good boy. His band was touring the States when he heard I was in here . . . "

"Right, Fa. But I still haven't heard what you did to land here."

Liza had wanted to ask this, but felt she mustn't.

There wasn't much to tell. Amos had worked on his boat all day, then he'd driven back to his digs in London and had blacked out on the stairs.

"They tell me I arrived here more or less dead." He shrugged and smiled bleakly.

"And dribbling nuts and bolts and rivets from every pocket," Liza added. They could laugh about it now. She looked at the clock and hastily said goodbye to the two men.

In the corridor she met Andrew. He smiled, and she thought for a moment he was going to stop and speak to her, but he went on to the nurse's station.

He's effecting me like a case of flu, she thought.

The lift had gone all the way to the sixth floor where it seemed to be permanently moored. She was about to start down the stairs when she saw Andrew coming back. Not wanting to appear to flee, she waited, pushing the DOWN button impatiently.

"I see you've been visiting our friend again," he observed.

"He's so nice," she murmured. "And until today he's had almost no visitors."

Andrew studied her a moment. Then he said, "Let's take the stairs. I've been wanting to speak to you."

He held the heavy fire door for her.

This echoing stairway always smelled strongly of disinfectant. They started down, and on the first landing Andrew grasped her wrist and turned her to face him.

"Trust me, Liza."

"Trust you? Why?" she whispered, bewildered.

Instead of answering, he bent his head suddenly and kissed her hard on her mouth. She tried to pull away, but his arms were around her, imprisoning her against him.

"You know why," he whispered, his lips on her cheek.

Her resistance weakened. She didn't want to break away. She didn't want to think about trust. She wanted only to remain in his embrace, on and on.

At last, he looked gravely into her eyes. "Do you remember that I made one promise to you?"

She knew immediately what promise he meant, for she had thought of it over and over, in spite of her conviction that it would never be kept.

"Yes, I remember," she murmured. Standing close to her in their secret grove, he had promised they would return.

"Do you want the promise to be kept?"

He was so close, his presence was intoxicating. She wanted to tell him how many times she had already returned in her thoughts. She looked up into his dark, questioning eyes.

"Do you?" he asked again, still more quietly.

She remembered her confusion and hurt when he hardly spoke to her after their return from Springbeck. What did he want — Martha Newman for his London lady and Liza for hill-walking?

Obviously, he wanted to carry on with Martha, and he seemed to think he could keep Liza's trust merely by asking for it.

How could she believe they'd ever go back. It was something to be remembered, not repeated.

"No," she whispered.

He looked at her a long moment. Then, without a word, walked quickly away.

6

THE foul weather matched Liza's mood as she swayed in the aisle of the crowded rush-hour bus. She'd just been interviewed for the post of relief nurse for a refugee camp in the Sudan. She could have signed the contract that same afternoon, but she'd have to start the end of the month.

"Relief is the operative word," the interviewer had said. "Some of our people have worked over a year without time off. We must have someone now. We can't wait until July. I'm very sorry, Miss Carter."

If only I hadn't tied myself up in Springbeck through June, she agonized. She was so distracted, she nearly rode past the hospital bus stop.

She stepped off the bus to be walloped head-on by wind-driven rain. With gusts billowing her coat and skirt before her, she was struggling toward St. Anne's main entrance when she hit a wet, unyielding object. She looked up and found herself in the arms of Bobby Harper.

"I've been trying to catch you," he laughed. "And now I've got you."

You have indeed, she thought. She had lost her balance, and he was all that kept her upright.

He took her arm and together they made the final dash to the entrance.

"Sister Robson mentioned you'd stopped by." Liza admitted.

"Understatement of the year! I keep on and on stopping by. Is it true that you spend all your waking hours scrubbed, sterile and inaccessible?" His voice was plaintive.

"Of course not. I have a half hour coffee break at about one thirty in the morning, and if I'm lucky, another one sometime later." She felt quite safe in admitting this.

"Aha," he looked so pleased, she wondered if she'd been foolish to mention her free time, after all, remembering he, too, was a night worker. She quickly changed the subject.

"If you're going to see your father, give him my regards. I'll probably see him later." She flashed him a smile and was about to hurry off.

"Don't you want to know why I was looking for you?" He sounded so disappointed, Liza felt ashamed of her brusque manner.

"Yes, of course I do."

He had wanted to thank her for her kindness to his father. He said, "Dad and I keep trying to think of some way to thank this whole wonderful staff for all they've done."

"It's what we're here for," Liza said. She always felt a little awkward with grateful patients or their families. "I'm so pleased he seems to be recovering."

"That's the other thing I wanted to ask you," Bobby said. "We've got to make some decisions about his boat. I thought, since he said you're a sailor, you might be able to advise me. Do you think he'll ever sail again?"

Liza sighed. "Do you sail yourself?"

"Put it this way — since I could walk, I've been press-ganged whenever my father couldn't find anyone better to crew for him."

"Then," Liza said, "You know how varied conditions can be. That has to be considered. But I can't advise you. You'll have to talk to the consultant."

She felt Amos's sailing days were over, but what would that leave him to fill his days — memories and old snap shots.

She said, "Could you put off decisions for a while?"

"That's what I'd do," Bobby said, "If I weren't going off to Australia in a few weeks."

"Do talk to the consultant," she said. "I wish I could be more help, but I really can't."

The Harpers' problems took Liza's mind off the Sudan until she went to the dining room.

There the houseman approached her with a broad smile and the advert about that post. He'd clipped it from the paper, certain he'd discovered just the thing for her. She thanked him but had to tell him about her discouraging interview.

As the houseman left to join the queue, she looked up and saw Andrew in the doorway. Her heart-beat turned staccato as he glanced toward her.

He stood a moment, looking around, then left.

Liza lingered over her beans and sausage, but he didn't come back. At least, Martha wasn't with him, she consoled herself.

Ready to leave, she spied Nurse Daniels carrying a tray toward her table. The old nurse said, "Don't let me keep you if you were on your way."

"You aren't keeping me. It's my slothful nature that does it." She leaned back in her chair.

"Rest while you can, my dear. It's

Friday, and you know what Casualty will be tonight — the usual weekend mayhem."

"Right. That calls for another cup of tea."

Liza had just returned to the table when Martha sat down beside Nurse Daniels. The old nurse peered at a small salad on her tray and exclaimed, "Is that your whole meal? It wouldn't keep a bird alive!"

Martha wrinkled her nose. "I can't stand the food here. It's almost pure carbohydrates. I'm not surprised half the nurses are overweight." She fussed at her salad, taking tiny bites.

Nurse Daniels gently pointed out that there wasn't an overweight nurse in sight at the moment.

"Those are probably the ones who smoke. A pack a day will keep the weight off nicely, mainly by rotting the lungs away."

"You're full of cheer tonight," Liza couldn't resist the remark, but Martha ignored it.

"Have you seen Andrew . . . Dr. Peterson?" she asked. "He usually comes in around this time."

Since her remarks were so clearly directed to Nurse Daniels, Liza said nothing.

Nurse Daniels said, "Perhaps he's off to Cumbria for the weekend. I've heard he's going to apply for his father's practice."

Martha put down her fork and looked at her two companions, acknowledging Liza's presence for the first time. "I dearly hope he's appointed." Her tone was ardent. "It's so right for him, and such a lovely place. I'd love to be going there."

Nurse Daniels asked, "Didn't I hear you're going to work for him?"

Liza's attention was galvanized.

Martha frowned. "No, I'm going to Paris to work with a friend of his for a few weeks next term."

"Yes, I know about that," Nurse Daniels said. "But I thought I heard one of you girls was going to Cumbria . . ."

Martha interrupted her, "I may be going up for a visit. I know Andrew's family, of course."

Liza didn't want to hear any more. She finished her tea, stood up and said to Nurse Daniels, "You've probably heard about me. I'm going to work with Dr. Peterson's father in June."

She left without waiting to see Martha's reaction. Regretting the time she'd wasted in the dining room, she felt cross with herself and everyone else.

There was still time for a visit to Amos.

She found changes. The bed beside Amos's was empty. Silence and deep gloom had replaced the usual cheery atmosphere of the room.

"I have to get out of here, Nurse Carter," Amos moaned. He lay back on his pillows, gazing up at her, his eyes red and sorrowful.

"You will. Why not wait 'til this rainy spell ends?"

While she tried to think what had

brought on this slump in his spirits, she saw Andrew, with the ward sister who appeared to be giving him worrisome news. However, he walked into the room smiling.

They hadn't spoken since she had callously rejected his promise. She felt she had blasted a chasm between them; and although she longed for communication, at the same time she dreaded it.

At first he seemed to ignore her, going directly to Amos. "Mr. Harper, how do you do it? I've never seen a man attract pretty nurses like you do."

Amos's two room-mates began showing a bit more animation. The younger one said, "It's him being a sailor that does it. A lot of women can't resist a sailor. Isn't that right, Nurse?"

"So I've heard." Liza smiled. At least, this was better than that awful apathy.

But Amos was not to be distracted.

"I want to get out of here," he repeated. "And I don't want to go the way poor old Howard went." He nodded at the empty bed beside his own.

The man opposite said, "They pulled the curtains around him in the night, and this morning when we woke he was gone — turned in his cards, he 'ad."

"Old Howard," sighed the other, "He thought he'd be going home soon to get his garden started."

"This happens," Andrew said, soberly, but in a matter-of-fact tone.

"Speaking of sailors," he said, deliberately changing the subject, "Does Nurse Carter know your sloop flys the Dunkirk flag?"

Liza looked at Amos with awe. "You never told me! Does that mean you helped evacuate the troops? You wouldn't have been old enough."

He nodded proudly. "My brother and I went. I was seventeen and he was a year younger, and SONGSTRESS was a new boat, then. She belonged to my uncle who was away in the Navy."

The atmosphere in the ward was much improved by the time Liza and Andrew left.

He looked at the clock as they passed the nurse's station. "Ah, I might still get something to eat."

Waiting for the lift, he said, "I'm worried about our friend, Amos."

"But he seemed to be doing so well!"

"The ward sister suspects he might be hiding his symptoms because he wants to go home so badly."

"Poor old man," Liza sighed. "That won't help matters."

"I don't think that crazy son of his is helping either."

Liza glanced quickly at Andrew, not sure she had heard him correctly.

"What do you mean?"

"The ward sister says he's been giving him a lot of unrealistic hopes that he'll be able to leave hospital soon and that he might still be able to sail."

"Well, maybe he can. Don't be

so gloomy. People do recover from coronaries, don't they?"

"You sound just like his son."

Liza put down her cup with a thud. "You can't know what he sounds like. You said you heard all this from the ward sister. Have you ever talked to Bobby Harper?"

She tried to sound calm and reasonable, but she heard her voice rising in spite of her efforts. "Andrew, you can't call him crazy when you don't know him at all!"

He looked up, startled by her fervour, "Do you know him so well?"

"No, but I'm not calling him crazy, either."

Andrew's eyes fastened upon her face. He sighed. "Liza, with your green eyes flashing under that tawny mane, you're a stirring sight."

"Oh, don't, Andrew." She hid her face in her hands.

"It's ironic," he mused. "Here we are arguing about Bobby Harper. I've been wanting to talk to you about us."

"Us?" Her heart missed a beat.

"In view of what you said last night, I have a better idea of how you feel about us. But we ought to try for a working relationship, a detente, for these next few weeks, don't you agree?"

She nodded morosely.

"Last night on the stairs . . . I let myself be diverted . . . " He smiled bleakly — "By your devilish attraction. And now tonight I've made you angry again."

She looked up and found him gazing at her rather grimly. Their eyes met.

The lift arrived.

Neither spoke on the way down to Casualty. Liza thought, we seem to be reaching for each other through a tangle of thorns.

* * *

For a Friday night, Casualty was exceptionally quiet. Even the usual influx of cuts and bruises, nose-bleeds, chesty babies and sick drunks had petered out after eleven. The work list was up to date, and Clare had actually run out of jobs. She, too, was idle and had been flicking through the pages of NURSING MIRROR when Liza complained about the lack of action.

"There's still time for plenty to happen," Clare reminded her as she opened a box of chocolates left by a grateful patient. She passed the box to Liza.

"I'm not in the mood for sweets, thank you."

"What's the matter, Liza?" Clare's voice was gentle. "Something has been bothering you, hasn't it?"

Liza shook her head. It would be comforting to tell her everything, as she always had done since the days when they were the only little girls at Willowbrook.

But what could she tell her? The boundaries between happy and unhappy had become blurred. Nothing was very right or very wrong.

"I don't know," she said. "I think

when I get my career going in the right direction, I'll be okay. It was disappointing, missing out on that job in the Sudan."

"The course in Liverpool . . . " Clare began.

"I know. I'm going to write to your cousin."

"I suppose you've seen these adverts?" Clare opened the MIRROR to the back pages and read, "The Gwelo General Hospital, Zimbabwe needs State Registered Nurses; Medic International wants SRN's for Belgium and France; King Abdulaziz University Hospital in Jeddah — two year contracts . . . "

"None would be as good as Assam or the Sudan. They're all in hospitals in big towns or cities. Besides, having to spend June in Springbeck will probably rule out anything I find now. And there's no hope that Springbeck will lead to anything."

"It would almost certainly lead to working for Dr. Peterson, if he takes over his father's practice."

"You know I don't want to go back to Cumbria to work."

"I also heard you say, not long ago, that you'd go anywhere on earth to work with Dr. Peterson. I thought you were quite smitten by him."

Liza sighed and ticked off on her fingers her reasons for changing her mind about following him.

"A — I never dreamed he would go back to Cumbria instead of Africa.

B — He's a very difficult man.

And C — . . . " Liza seemed to have forgotten C.

"And C, Martha Newman has you convinced she owns him," Clare finished for her.

"In itself," Liza said, "That wouldn't matter, if he were going to take me to Africa with him. I don't need a man. I need a job."

Clare sighed, as though relieved of a worry. "Then, you haven't been moping around because you're falling for the good doctor."

Liza gazed mournfully at her friend. "I can't be in love with anyone, Clare. You know what I want to do. As far back as I can remember, I've aimed to do what my Grandmother did. I have to stay independent to do that. I don't even want to consider the possibility of falling in love."

"It isn't the sort of thing one considers," Clare laughed. "It just happens."

"Well, it won't happen to me for a while. I have more important things to do." She thought, if this isn't completely true at the moment, it doesn't matter. I'm going to make it be true.

"If that's how you feel, then being in love is definitely not your problem, because when you're in love, nothing is more important."

"So I've heard. But I'm not convinced that . . . " She was interrupted by the porter.

"I have someone here looking for Nurse Carter," he said. "She's on duty tonight, isn't she?"

Liza rose and went around the desk. "Ah, there you are, Nurse Carter."

He beckoned to someone by the door. Liza was surprised to see Bobby Harper standing there, clutching a huge white box.

He hurried to the desk and presented the box to Liza. "Chocolate eclairs," he announced. "To have at your one thirty coffee break, plenty for everybody."

Both girls were speechless. Clare was the first to recover from her astonishment. Naturally gracious, her immediate impulse was to invite him to join them in the canteen.

"You must come and enjoy this lovely treat with us."

"I'd love it," he said. "But I've a taxi waiting. I'm on duty, too, THE BLUEBLOODS are playing at the Roundelay Club. This is the interval."

Liza was touched. "Bobby, you've gone to such trouble. How kind of you."

He dismissed it as nothing and

handed her an envelope. "Here are some tickets, if anyone would like to come hear THE BLUEBLOODS."

Before they could thank him, he had glanced at his watch and made a dash for the door. "See you, then," he called.

7

LIZA was in her room on Sunday afternoon, finally going through the prospectus from Liverpool, when she heard the hall telephone ringing.

"Let it be Andrew," she whispered.

But how ridiculous, she thought. He's most likely occupied with Martha. She listened for footsteps. Wouldn't anyone answer? Was she the only one sitting in her room on this lovely afternoon?

She jumped up, and to make up for her delay, ran down the hall, reaching the phone the moment it stopped ringing. It could just possibly have been Andrew, she thought, tormenting herself. If it was, he didn't ring again. And he wasn't in the dining room when she dashed over for a quick supper at six thirty.

She went up to see Amos. She hadn't seen him since Bobby had treated the department to Eclairs. He'd be pleased to hear how much they'd been enjoyed in the canteen.

Two student nurses were chatting with him. They'd been to the Roundelay club. The old man all but purred as they raved about THE BLUEBLOODS and Bobby's drumming.

When Liza entered they turned to go.

"Don't leave," she exclaimed. "I want to hear about them, too."

A few minutes later the students were obviously thrilled when Bobby, himself, came in.

Liza stayed longer than she'd intended. After a day alone in her room, she enjoyed chatting with the Harpers.

When she left, Bobby walked her to the lifts. He told her the consultant had advised him to make no decisions about the boat until it was absolutely necessary.

Back at the Residence, she found a

mass of glittering, rain-drop studded daffodils wrapped in wet newspapers and propped against her door. She raised them to her face to inhale their fragrance and saw that the paper was the CARLISLE HERALD. "Oh Andrew!" she murmured.

Monday night Liza tried not to notice that Andrew spent every spare minute holed up in the doctor's room with Martha. They were going through records for some kind of report she was writing.

If she does less than brilliantly, it won't be for lack of help, Liza thought. Andrew looked almost fatherly, as he sat explaining things to her. Why is he so kind and patient to her and so rough with me, she wondered sadly.

She didn't have a chance to thank him for the daffodils until they were going off duty in the morning.

He fell in step beside Liza.

She said, "They're from Springbeck, aren't they? It must have been dreamy there in this nice weather."

"I haven't been home. Mother brought them for you. She was here for the weekend, shopping for her trip. She tried to contact you to have Sunday dinner with us. You must have been out."

Liza remembered the phone call she'd missed. Somebody up there hates me, she thought.

Andrew said, "I've been wanting to tell you . . . I'm concerned about your taking over for my mother in June — I don't want you to feel obligated to come if something better should turn up."

She thought bitterly, he's a little late with that, but he couldn't have known about the job in the Sudan.

Maybe the Petersons had decided they didn't want her, after all? "Have you found someone better?"

She wished she didn't sound so belligerent, but she was shocked that he'd expect her to renege on her promise to his mother.

When she headed toward the

courtyard, he stayed with her and held the door for her. They were both struck by the beauty of the morning.

Raindrops sparkled on the ivy that climbed this side of the old nurses' home, and the sun sucked up steamy little clouds from pavement puddles. Liza felt her indignation evaporate, too. They stood by the door, breathing in the lovely freshness.

Andrew had not answered her question; but without resentment she said, "I promised your mother I'd come, and unless she wants someone else, I'll be there."

He persisted. "There would still be time if . . ."

"Andrew, are you trying to tell me I'm not wanted?"

They were strolling toward her entrance, but now Andrew stopped and turned to glare at her.

"Don't you understand? I feel that you might have taken the job with unrealistic expectations of one kind or another. I want to give you a chance to change your mind if you'd like to."

For a moment she wanted to tell him she'd already thrown away a chance to work in the Sudan, but that wouldn't be fair. It had been her own choice to honour her commitment. She couldn't blame that on him. What good would it do, anyway.

But UNREALISTIC EXPECT-ATIONS! That made her hackles rise. She wasn't sure whether he meant expectations about his devotion to her or about a chance of a foreign job with him in the future.

Grimly, she recognized that either would have been unrealistic, but that, indeed, she had once hoped for both. She couldn't endure the indignity of his knowing this.

"You'll never win any medals for tact," she grumbled.

"Speaking of tact, Liza, I don't think you take any prizes either — blethering in the canteen about coming to Springbeck."

"I never . . . " She stopped short,

remembering how she had flaunted the information in front of Martha. "Is that embarrassing to you for some reason?"

Two students came running down the steps, obviously late, and nearly collided with Andrew. They apologized and ran on laughing.

"There's not much use in continuing this conversation." His tone was frigid.

Liza sadly shook her head. Her eyes met and beseeched his, and for a moment he seemed about to speak. He turned away instead, and she watched him walk across the bright courtyard, his shadow long in the slanting morning sunlight.

She wanted desperately not to care what was happening to them; but I do care, she thought, and I don't know what to do about it. Forlornly, she made her way up the worn stone steps.

"Hi!" The cheery voice belonged to the student midwife, waiting on the top step, grinning. "I do like your style, Nurse Carter."

"What on earth do you mean?" Her remark made no sense at all to Liza whose self esteem was at an all-time low.

"St. Anne's most devastating young doctor walks you home where you receive word that Bobby Harper, idol of thousands, wishes to speak with you. How do you do it? I'd like lessons, if you ever had a few free minutes."

The student's good humoured teasing raised her spirits. She smiled. "You took a message for me?"

"You just missed his phone call. I left a note with a number under your door. The dear man said it's urgent."

She rang him even before going to her room, but there was no answer. She tried again an hour later and again when she awoke in the afternoon, still without success. I'll catch him while he's visiting his father, she thought, wondering what could have been so urgent that morning.

Since it was too early for visiting

Amos, she sat down at her desk and wrote to Liverpool for the application forms for the Community Health Course. If they would have her, it was probably what she should do, all things considered.

* * *

Getting that letter written was a relief. Indecision had been wearing her down. She thought she felt better already, as she stuck a stamp on the envelope — for better or for worse.

She selected a few of the fattest daffodils to take to Amos, picked up her letter, and set off.

She found Amos's bed empty.

"What's become of him?" her voice betrayed her anxiety.

"He took an awful turn this morning," his room-mate's tone was dismal. "They took him off somewhere. I can't tell you anything more."

She found him back in the Coronary Care Unit with Bobby, Andrew and the

146

Medical Consultant, crowded around him.

Amos smiled at her. The macabre green light of the ECG made all of them look like zombies, but Liza was distressed to see the dark circles under the old man's sunken eyes. She was alarmed at his look of resignation.

No one spoke to her, but Andrew moved away to make room for her beside him.

Amos said, "You two were standing together like that, only smiling, when I came back. Remember, in the lift . . . ?"

He had to rest after the effort of speaking. After a minute, he said, "Where's Bobby." He reached out.

"Here I am, Fa." Bobby put his hand in his father's.

The old man weakly carried it to his lips and closed his eyes. Everyone else moved quietly out of the small room.

Impulsively, their quarrels forgotten, Liza turned to Andrew for comfort. He put his arm around her and she leaned against him a moment as they shared the weight of their sorrow.

She knew that, for whatever reason, Andrew had not been any more successful than she at maintaining what was called professional detachment in this case.

Later in the evening, Bobby came down to Casualty to thank them for what they'd done for his father and to say goodbye.

He told them Amos would be buried in Scotland beside his wife. He didn't tell Liza why he had phoned that morning. She supposed the call was about Amos.

The following Sunday she was surprised to have a call from him. He said he was on his way back from Scotland.

"Would you have dinner with me tonight? I'm verging on lonely." The cavalier tone was still there, but considerably subdued.

"Of course, I will. It will be good to see you."

She had never expected to hear from him again, which, she thought, would be quite all right. But now that he had contacted her in his loneliness, she couldn't refuse to see him, though she wondered why members of the band couldn't supply the emotional support he needed.

"I should warn you, I have ulterior motives," he went on. "I'm going to ask you a favour."

"Ask away," she hoped her voice didn't reveal the apprehension she felt.

"Not until I see you. I'll aim for eight, but I'm in Kent."

"How can you be in Kent if you're coming from Scotland. Did you get lost?"

"I'm in the boatyard, working on SONGSTRESS. All will be disclosed when I see you, which will be as soon as possible."

"Don't worry about the time. Sunday night traffic out there will be heavy. I'll be right here all the rest of the day."

When he turned up a little after

eight, she suggested they eat at a place she knew behind the hospital — a quiet neighbourhood restaurant, in no way festive.

As they entered the dimly lit foyer, a young couple on their way out stopped, whispered together briefly, and followed them in to ask shyly for Bobby's autograph.

Liza liked the friendly, modest way he complied. The two young fans were delighted.

"I don't ordinarily hobnob with celebrities," Liza observed after the fawning maitre d' had left them.

Bobby's smile was brief. He put down his menu, breathed deeply and squared his shoulders, as though steeling himself. He leaned close to Liza, and in a tone devoid of his usual playfulness, he said, "I don't think you ordinarily hobnob with married men, either."

Too surprised to answer, she merely shook her head.

They sat in silence while a waiter put down their drinks. At last Bobby said,

"In view of what I'm going to ask of you, I thought you should know my status." He paused and seemed to be watching Liza's reactions to what he was saying.

"Thank you for being honest with me. What is it you're going to ask?"

"Will you help me deliver SONG-STRESS to my uncle in France?"

She leaned back in her chair with great relief. "When?"

She could see from Bobby's grin how glad he was to get on to this less painful subject.

"When," he repeated. "That isn't easy to answer. I'll soon be going to Australia with THE BLUEBLOODS. It means fitting the voyage in as soon as the boat is ready. I'm hiring the work done and they've promised to move as fast as they can."

He told her a little about repairs the old boat needed, adding, "My Uncle Robert's along in years, too. Though he wants the boat, he won't be able to work on her himself."

He spent the rest of the evening talking about his father. Sensing how necessary this was for him, Liza encouraged him.

She learned that he and his father had been especially close, since Bobby was only a child when his mother died. Amos had adored her and had never thought of remarrying.

Regretfully, Bobby told of his father's disappointment that his own marriage had broken up.

"He liked my wife and always expected we'd get back together. We've never been divorced."

Liza noticed a change in his mood, from one of sadness to one of stressful frustration. He fingered his glass restlessly.

"We'll probably never live together again. But neither will we be divorced. We fight about everything, and yet I've never been able to want anyone else, and she's the same. We see each other now and then. It's why I keep the flat. I keep hoping. Maybe she does, too."

Any apprehension Liza felt about him vanished. She need not fear that their friendship could lead to complications. He would want nothing she was unwilling to give.

Bobby laid his hand on hers. "Forgive me. I've gone on about my family and my troubles. That's not what we're here to talk about." He squeezed her hand and smiled. "What do you think about our sail? It should be fun, don't you think?"

Before she could answer, someone said, "What will be fun?"

They both looked up and found Clare and Simon, grinning happily. They made room for them and introduced Simon.

"We're going to sail to France!" Liza announced.

They sat talking until the dining room closed, and it was almost eleven before Bobby left Liza at her door. When she flicked on the light in her room, she found a note had been pushed under her door. She recognized

Andrew's writing.

Mother's trip is cancelled. Please ring me when you return.

She sat on her bed, gazing at the few scrawled lines, wondering what could have happened. Was one of his parents ill? In her mind's eye she saw them waving goodbye to her the day she left Springbeck. Her concern about them crowded out other thoughts as she headed toward the hall telephone.

On her way, it occurred to her — she could have gone to the Sudan, after all; but of course, it would be too late now; the position would already be filled.

When she rang Casualty, she learned Andrew was on second call. It was eleven thirty. He was probably sleeping. She decided not to bother him.

As she lay unable to sleep, concern about the Petersons gave way to concern about her own situation.

She would indeed be out on the streets if she didn't find something quickly. She could stay with Clare or even join her mother in Scotland,

154

but what an anticlimax, after the ambitions she'd had. She'd rather take any temporary job she could find.

Niggling at the back of her mind, was the realization that she'd soon be cut off entirely from Andrew, now that she wouldn't be working in Springbeck. The image of their secret grove kept muddling her thoughts. She had to remind herself that there was no reason why she should want to see him.

Unable to contact him during the day, she didn't learn until evening what had happened. She saw him coming through the queue in the dining room.

He must have spent the weekend outdoors, for he was freshly tanned. His dark eyes and shining dark hair seemed to sparkle with vigour, which only gave Liza cause for annoyance. Why couldn't he be ordinary, instead of so incomparable.

She looked around for Martha. She hadn't yet arrived, but it was still early. The next time she looked up from her plate, Andrew was approaching her table. Their eyes met. She forced herself to remain expressionless.

Without asking if he might join her, he unloaded his tray at the place opposite her. "You found my note?"

"About Springbeck? Yes, I did."

"We're concerned about how this will effect you." His face was grave. He didn't start eating, but gave Liza his full attention.

"We want to do all we can to help you find something else. Mother tried to phone you as soon as we knew . . . "

"Knew what," Liza could wait no longer to hear what had happened.

"You haven't had her letter yet?" He frowned.

"Only your note."

"Of course! There was no post yesterday."

Liza wanted to appear indifferent, but she wasn't succeeding.

"Then you haven't heard about Virginia?" He didn't wait for an answer. "She telephoned us on Saturday. She's coming home. Her husband decided to pack it in. They'll be back soon."

"So — no trip for your mother." Liza was relieved to find that nothing had happened to either of the older Petersons.

Andrew said, "She almost bought her plane ticket when she was in London, but put it off; so all she's stuck with is her new travel clothes, which she doesn't mind a bit. The gifts she bought for Virginia will be welcome home presents.

"We're delighted for Virginia and for ourselves, but when we thought of you . . . "

Liza could imagine Mrs. Peterson, wringing her hands and telling Andrew something would have to be done about poor Liza. Dr. Peterson, too, would be upset that she'd have to change her plans so suddenly.

But for Andrew, she supposed this was a convenient way of easing her out of his life. He had so obviously found her less loveable than the naive girl he had taken home with him on that lovely day in early spring.

When she looked up and met his concerned blue eyes, she said, "Don't worry. It was only going to be for a month, anyway. There are plenty of that kind of jobs around."

She glanced beyond him and saw Clare standing at the end of the counter, looking for a place to sit. Seeing Liza, she started toward her, but when she saw who was with her she hesitated. Liza waved and beckoned. She didn't want to be alone with Andrew.

"Dr. Peterson!" Clare exclaimed. "It's not fair that you go heavenly bronze in the sun while I go lobster pink. Is that a Cumbria suntan?"

He nodded. "Partly, and partly motorway, driving with the top down yesterday afternoon."

Liza was having trouble with her emotions again. She remembered so well the feel of wind and sun beating down on them in the Morgan. She wondered if Martha had been sitting in her place yesterday.

Clare said, "I hear you might be in Springbeck full time pretty soon."

"Not so soon," Andrew said. "The practice won't be advertised until midsummer. Then it will be up to the committee to decide which applicant gets it."

He and Clare talked about Cumbria through the rest of the meal. Liza didn't join in, and finally, as though to bring her into the conversation, Clare said, "Has Dr. Peterson heard about your sailing adventure?"

She shook her head, wishing Clare had not mentioned it, especially when she noticed the doctor's keen interest.

"What sailing adventure?" He asked Clare, not Liza.

Clare said, "Bobby Harper is going to sail his father's boat to France. Liza's going to crew for him."

Andrew turned to Liza, his eyes flashing. "Are you?"

She nodded.

"Just the two of you?"

"As far as I know."

"Do you think this is wise, Liza?"

Clare had never heard him use her first name. She looked from one to the other, puzzled.

Before Liza could answer him, his bleeper sounded. He turned it off, glared at her and left, saying, "I want to talk to you about this."

"Did I say something wrong?" Clare asked.

Liza shook her head dejectedly.

Her friend was mystified. "He seemed awfully bothered about something."

Trying to pretend she didn't care, Liza said, "He often finds something to be cross about when I'm around."

"It was my fault." Clare was repentant. "I shouldn't have joined you; and maybe I shouldn't have told him you're going to France with Bobby. Was that the trouble?"

"Don't worry, Clare. It isn't important."

"You've really gone off him, haven't you!"

To avoid answering, Liza announced she wouldn't be going to Springbeck. When she had told about Virginia's return, Clare asked, "Is that why you're upset with Dr. Peterson?"

"Of course not. No one is to blame; and I'm not upset with him." She saw that Clare had finished. "Let's go."

Clare looked thoughtful, making no move to go. She said, "He can be so nice. Yet, I think Bobby Harper is more your type. He's always fun and good company."

Liza stood up, suddenly and impatiently. "Clare, they're both nice, but I don't need a man, remember?"

Clare shook her head in doubt. "So now, what about a job?"

"I have nothing lined up. Next week I'll be unemployed and of no fixed abode — truly a vagabond. Sounds interesting, doesn't it?"

"If it comes to that, I told you, you can stay with me." Clare looked at her watch. "I must phone Simon. Let's go."

Admissions through Casualty had been rising since the good weather began. As Nurse Daniels observed, "The minute spring arrives, Londoners rush outdoors looking for daft ways to get hurt. And it's us who get them," she lamented.

She and Liza were struggling to clean and dress a superficial laceration across the sole of an active two-year-old.

"What was a child like this doing outside at this hour, and without shoes?" she muttered.

Liza didn't have time to speculate. The student nurse was beside her saying, "Dr. Peterson needs you. I'll help Nurse Daniels."

Liza sighed. "Where is he?"

As she turned to go, she saw him waiting for her in the doorway. She followed him silently. They spent the next two hours together, working on a badly burned fireman. The task of dressing his wounds took their full attention. It was three in the morning before they finished.

Revived by an icy coke that Clare brought her, she was about to make a bed check when Dr. Peterson called her into the doctor's room. He pushed the door closed, directed her to the only chair and perched on the edge of the cluttered table.

"Liza, what's this nonsense about you sailing to France with Bobby Harper?"

Suddenly her energy drained away. She couldn't cope with this. What right had he to interfere in her affairs. She said, "We're on duty, Dr. Peterson. I was about to . . . "

"This won't take long. I just want to advise you as strongly as I can not to make that trip."

Liza hoped that silence on her part might bring this interview to a quick end. Of course, she'd make the trip, but she wouldn't talk about it with Andrew.

"Liza, I know much more about Amos Harper's boat than you think I do, and about his son, too."

"Ohhh, spare me this," Liza moaned.

But Andrew continued. "I've also sailed in the channel. It's no place for novices. Do you suppose Bobby can navigate well enough to make his landfall in France, let alone keep out of trouble on the way?"

"He'll do well enough, I'm sure."

"Well enough if you become fog-bound or have to make port in the dark?"

Liza wasn't certain of this herself, and she had carefully avoided thinking about it.

"Aside from problems the weather and channel currents can bring, there's the boat itself." Seeing Liza was about to rise, he moved to the door and stood with his back against it.

He went on, "Amos was worried about all the work it was beginning to need. It's an old boat . . . "

"Bobby is having the work done. And Amos considered it a fine old boat, Andrew."

She was beginning to see that he

really felt anxious for her safety. She didn't want this from him, but neither could she be angry at him for it.

"Please don't worry. There's no need." She smiled and stood up.

"Sit down." It was a command.

Andrew's face was suddenly grim. "I didn't want to tell you this. I hoped you would give up the trip if I pointed out how dangerous it could be. There's another thing to be considered.

"You ought to know that Bobby Harper is a married man. I presume he hasn't admitted this. His father told me in confidence. I'm only telling you now because I want to try to keep you from being hurt or hurting his wife."

"I happen to know all about Bobby's marriage. I suspect I know a good bit more than you do about it. So, if you don't mind . . . " She started toward the door.

She became aware of a change in Andrew. His face was pale as he came close to her. He grasped her shoulders roughly.

His face close to hers, he gazed at her with an expression of utter disgust. She looked at his lips and wanted them, even at that moment. He dropped his hands and turned away. In a tight, expressionless voice, he said, "You'd better get out of here."

8

"IT'S going to be a rough night," Clare predicted, and Liza soon discovered what she meant.

Ward C was already full; there was a patient in every cubicle; wheel chairs and beds clogged the corridor outside X-ray, and the waiting room was packed.

Seeing Andrew come out of a treatment room with Martha, she walked quickly in the opposite direction. He'd be on second call, and with any luck, she might be able to avoid him.

Clare asked her to help the orthopaedic registrar, and he kept her busy for the next few hours.

Not wanting to have to talk to anyone, she worked through her break, then wished she had gone to the canteen, after all, because Andrew came into the office while she was filling a case report.

He said nothing, and she kept her face averted, but she decided they couldn't go on like this.

In the morning she'd write him a letter explaining once and for all that she wanted nothing from Bobby, and that he had never wanted anything from her except her help in delivering the boat.

Their paths didn't cross again during the hectic night; and back in her room, exhausted though she was, Liza sat down to write the letter. But why, she asked herself, should I have to explain anything to him. She tore up the half-finished note, took a long shower and went to bed.

When she woke after a short, troubled sleep, she found the letter from Mrs. Peterson, whose remorse at having to tell Liza she wouldn't be needed was obviously genuine. She closed with an invitation to revisit Springbeck. "You and Virginia would get on like a house afire, and the rest of us would so enjoy seeing you again."

The rest of you minus one, Liza thought. Sadly, this was an invitation that would never be accepted. She wrote a short, friendly, evasive letter and went out to buy stamps. When she returned, the hall phone was ringing.

Bobby sounded breathless. "Time is short. We leave for Australia sooner than I thought. Can we make our voyage this Saturday?"

Liza thought he knew she'd be on duty. "Only if I can talk Clare and the Supervisor into letting me off. I'd have to find someone to work for me."

"Do you want to look into that and call me back tonight."

Liza agreed. "I'd have to ask for Sunday, too, wouldn't I?"

Bobby thought a minute. "I suppose so, to be on the safe side. Even if we're back early enough, you'd be tired."

"What this means is that I'll leave my job two days sooner. Sunday was to be my last night. I'll see what I can do."

"Wait," Bobby said. "There's something else. This is surprising, I thought. I had a phone call from Dr. Peterson."

Liza gasped. "What on earth did he want?"

"He knew we'd be taking SONGSTRESS to France soon. I suppose he heard about it from you. He said my father had spoken so often of the boat, and that he'd promised him a sail someday."

Liza waited breathlessly. "Is that what he wanted?"

"He asked if he could come along to France."

"And what did you say?"

"What could I say? I hope you don't mind. It might turn out to be useful to have a third hand, and he seemed a nice enough chap when I've met him around the hospital. A bit aloof, perhaps, but Fa thought he was . . ."

"So he's going," Liza interrupted. She failed to hide the indignation she felt.

170

"You'd rather it was just the two of us?"

She was at a loss to answer that. She couldn't ask Bobby not to take him, especially in view of Andrew's assertion that Amos had promised him a sail.

But what was this going to be — out in a small boat with Andrew and Bobby for eight hours or longer? She couldn't begin to imagine such a situation. What nerve Andrew had, to ask to go along. But Bobby was waiting for her answer.

"We don't even know if I can get the weekend off yet," she reminded him. Then she was struck by the thought that Andrew, too, would be on duty. They were on the same rota.

"Does Dr. Peterson know you plan to go this weekend?"

"I was going to call him as soon as I talked to you."

"Well, I can tell you, he's also on duty." She thought, if I can get off and he can't, all will be well again.

"I'll see what he says, and we'll talk later."

★ ★ ★

Judging from the queue of patients and relatives outside Clare's office, it would be a while before Liza could talk about the weekend. On her way to Ward C, she saw Andrew through the open door of the doctor's room. Martha was with him, showing him X-rays which she held up to the light. She watched them stroll into the corridor, still so absorbed in their discussion they didn't even see her.

She interrupted them, saying, "Dr. Peterson, may I have a word with you?"

Andrew responded as she should have expected. He glanced up, his face expressionless.

"Later, Nurse Carter."

He hadn't broken his stride. Martha hadn't looked her way.

Nurse Daniels, hurrying out of

Ward C, seeing Liza's dejected look, smiled and winked at her. "They're trying to kill us with work again tonight," she muttered as she passed.

She worked through her first break and didn't have a chance to take her second one until after four when she felt she had used up her last ounce of energy.

Finding the canteen empty, she tipped back her chair and closed her eyes to wait for her coffee to cool. The warmth of the room, the whirr and gurgle of the machines and the blessed isolation created a strangely pleasant atmosphere, a womb-like refuge, very different than when the room was filled with chattering, white-coated staff.

At the sound of footsteps in the corridor she opened her eyes. Andrew was coming through the door.

"You wanted to see me," he stated.

"Not so urgently you had to come looking for me at this hour of the night."

"It's all right. I'm waiting for lab results."

When she continued to gaze into her coffee cup, he said, "I presume it was not about a patient."

She suddenly wanted desperately to make him understand. Without planning how she would do it, she said, "Andrew, you were mistaken about Bobby and me. We aren't even very close friends — just friendly acquaintances, really.

"His intentions couldn't be more honourable. Before he asked me if I'd sail to France with him, he made a point of letting me know he had a wife. I don't know what Amos might have told you about them, but they do have troubles and they don't live together."

Without looking up, she said, "I haven't anything more to say, Andrew; except that I'm not going to France if you're going."

"Suit yourself," he said, and he left.

She phoned Bobby and told him,

"I'm sorry, I'm not going with you, after all."

"They won't let you off?" He sounded disappointed.

"I haven't asked. It's just that I have a lot to do, what with my job ending. And you don't need two of us. I saw Dr. Peterson, and I understand he's going."

Bobby was silent a minute; then he said, "I was looking forward to having you along. I'm sorry."

"I'm sorry, too. But thank you for asking me, Bobby."

She put the phone back slowly and stood, leaning against the wall, feeling cold and empty. She could see hardly any prospect of happiness in the present or the future. She sighed and returned to her room. Her next problem was finding a job quickly. She still had to make a living.

Though her bed looked irresistible, she had to stay up to call the nurses' registry.

"Come in on Monday," the woman

suggested when Liza said she was ready to take almost anything that was temporary and provided accommodation.

That night she had no choice but to work with Andrew. Along with the usual Friday night influx to Casualty, came a score of bruised and lacerated victims of a coach crash. Everyone worked like automatons, hour after hour, and personal feelings had no place in the night's work.

Liza found that she and Andrew could still function competently as a team. When they were through with the last case, they walked away from each other; and remembering he would leave on SONGSTRESS in the morning, she realized she had worked with him for the last time. They weren't even going to say goodbye.

After his tiring night, she suspected Andrew would spend as much of the day as possible in a bunk, unless, of course, he was too worried about Bobby's seamanship to trust him alone on deck. It was hard to imagine how he and Bobby would act toward each other during their long day's sail.

Clare, who had already heard that Andrew would go to France instead of Liza, said, as they prepared to hand over to the day staff, "There's a lovely pink dawn. Are you sorry you aren't going with Bobby?"

Liza knew she was fishing for an explanation for the change of plans. Maybe some other time she would tell her the whole sad story, but it was still too painful to discuss. Right now, she had to ask her friend a favour, one she'd hoped she'd never have to ask.

Clare said, "Of course, you'll stay with me between jobs. I'm expecting you to help me get ready for the house-warming party. On my own I can't possibly have the flat ready."

Liza gave her a quick hug. "It will only be for a day or two. Can I come Monday morning?"

On Saturday night, unlike the weather which worsened during the evening, the Casualty Department enjoyed a blessed lull.

"It's because we admitted all of London last night," Nurse Daniels explained. "There's nobody left out there to get into trouble."

Yes, there is, Liza thought. There are two men in a small boat, and the sky was red at morning — sailors take warning.

She had been wakened at noon by her curtains billowing in what she reckoned to be a Force 8 gale. When she closed her window and wiped the wet sill, she peered out at a slate grey sky. She hoped Bobby had heard the shipping forecast and stayed in port.

It worried her that the sky had been so deceptively clear when she'd gone to bed that morning. She had missed the weather report, but her own prediction had been that it would be a great day for sailing, in spite of the pink dawn.

It was from Martha that she learned when Andrew and Bobby had planned to set out. "They were going to leave around six this morning," she was telling anyone who cared to listen as they sat over leisurely coffees on this very slow evening.

Liza wondered what reason Andrew would give Martha for his sudden decision to sail to France. She didn't have to wonder long.

Nurse Daniels asked the precise question, and Martha announced that the owner of a yacht was stuck for crew.

"Andrew feared he wasn't experienced enough to sail across the Channel alone, so he went along to help out."

Liza felt her hackles rise. Her very existence had been cancelled out. Bobby wouldn't have had to sail alone. Andrew knew she planned to go with him until he had interfered.

She was about to leave; but Martha's next remark stunned her into immobility.

She said, "Besides, there's no more need for him to run up to Cumbria every free weekend, now that his brother-in-law is taking over."

Nurse Daniels said, "Does that mean he won't apply for his father's practice?"

"Not this year." Martha looked around, as though to survey her audience. She obviously enjoyed being the authority on everything pertaining to Andrew.

Liza waited, tense and breathless.

"They expect to get approval for his brother-in-law to do a year's vocational traineeship in the practice, so Andrew's father won't be retiring yet. It's all just been decided in the past week."

Liza closed her eyes, trying to comprehend the total implications of what she'd heard. What would Andrew do now?

Again, Nurse Daniels asked her question for her. But this time, Martha's answer was vague.

"He's undecided, I think. When we were in Springbeck last weekend, he told his father he had several tempting possibilities, but it was too early to talk about them."

The houseman and the registrar joined them and the speculation about Andrew's future was dropped.

"We're running on the generators," the houseman reported. "The whole neighbourhood is blacked out; wires are down everywhere, they say. The storm is getting worse."

"It's that time of year," the registrar observed.

Please let SONGSTRESS be tied up on one or the other side of the Channel, Liza prayed. She didn't even know the direction of the wind. If it veered east, and Bobby had to beat into it, they might still be trying to make port. And she wondered just how well Amos's old boat could take heavy seas.

Her worries for the safety of SONGSTRESS and her crew were set aside when she heard Martha going on about last weekend's perfect weather in Cumbria.

"We rode both ways with the top down."

The young student couldn't have known the effect her words had on one member of her audience.

Liza put down her cup to hide the trembling of her hands. She sat deathly still until she had full control, then she turned to Martha.

"Excuse me," she was pleased at how calm she sounded. "I heard you mention that you'd been to Springbeck. Do you know if Andrew brought back my slacks and shoes?"

All conversation at the table stopped. The registrar laughed. "Do you girls take turns with the good doctor?"

"Well done, Dr. Peterson," the houseman hooted.

Martha went pale. "I have no idea," she mumbled.

"Oh well, I should have reminded him." She left as laughter continued behind her. That wasn't very nice of me, she thought.

She was scanning the work list, looking for a job that would keep her mind off everything but the immediate task, when Nurse Daniels sidled up to her.

"You're worried about that boat out in the storm, aren't you?"

Her words made the situation sound terrifying.

"Slightly," Liza admitted. "How did you know?"

The old nurse looked away. "I thought something had to be upsetting you. It's not like you to be unkind."

"Was I?" Liza knew she was behaving badly.

"Don't try to pull the wool over my eyes, Liza. I've been watching young people around St. Anne's too long for that. It's too bad. You two could be friends just as well, you know."

"I don't need friends."

"Have you ever thought that maybe Martha does?" Her face was grave and her voice serious. "She's had a hard life, you know."

Liza remembered Nurse Daniels telling her of Martha being orphaned.

I'm sorry about that, she thought, but it doesn't give her a license to . . . To what? what is it she does to annoy me? She had to face it; her sin was to be preferred by Andrew.

"I'm not being very nice." This time she said it aloud, and with genuine regret.

"You are nice. You just have your moments, like all of us."

"I won't be nasty again. But I'm afraid we aren't likely to be great chums either."

"I don't know why she's so awkward at making friends," Nurse Daniels murmured.

Liza couldn't resist saying, "She's certainly won over Dr. Peterson."

"That's different, of course. They were practically related."

"What do you mean?" All Liza's attention focussed on Nurse Daniels. Could it be that Andrew and Martha's relationship was different than she had suspected?

"I mean, after all, her sister was his fiancée."

Liza was speechless.

Suddenly, it all made sense. Here was the link between Andrew and Martha which Liza should have guessed at weeks ago. How had she overlooked the fact that the photograph of Flora she had seen in Springbeck could have been a photo of Martha: they so resembled each other. It must have been Flora's dark hair that threw her off.

How could Andrew help but be hypnotized by Martha? He must feel that he has his lost love back again.

Nurse Daniels still stood beside her, ostensibly reading the work list.

Liza silently mulled over what she'd just heard. She said, "I'm glad you set me straight, Nurse Daniels. Thank you."

She heard people coming back from the canteen. "I'd better get to work before Clare catches me skiving. I don't want to get the sack on my next to last night."

Just before dawn, she walked out onto the tarmac to try to detect the wind's direction, which was almost impossible to do among the tall buildings. She did think its strength had diminished.

On Sunday the hall phone woke her several times, but the calls weren't for her. Although Bobby hadn't promised to call when he returned, she thought he might suspect that she'd be concerned. Andrew, of course, wouldn't call. She was sure of that.

And he didn't turn up at work Sunday night. That was not alarming, in itself. Liza knew Bobby had allowed for the possibility of getting back late.

On Monday morning, after loading her few possessions into Clare's car, she left St. Anne's Infirmary as unobtrusively as she had come. She settled into Clare's guest bed, not because she was particularly tired, but because Clare had to get her sleep and Liza didn't want to disrupt her hostess's routine.

She wanted to try to call Bobby. She

still had a gnawing anxiety about him and Andrew. But she resisted. If he had reached home late Sunday night, he wouldn't appreciate her waking him just to ask how he was.

She crept out quietly for her appointment at the registry. She'd taken Clare's key, so she could let herself in, but as she entered Clare came yawning out of her bedroom, blinking in the bright daylight.

"What did they have to offer?" she asked.

"Nothing exciting. Lots of private duty, several locums in psychiatric nursing and geriatrics. I'm going back tomorrow. They think they'll have something in paediatrics."

"Liza why don't you wait until next week. You need a little time off before taking another job. You don't have to rush into anything."

"You wouldn't want me underfoot a whole week."

"I told you — I need you. With the party coming up Friday and the flat in the state it's in, you could make all the difference."

Liza looked around at the half stripped woodwork. The walls of the small foyer were a collage of half peeled wallpaper. "But you're taking off a week, aren't you?"

"I won't be off until Wednesday: and then, right after the party, Simon and I go to Willowbrook to make final arrangements for the wedding."

They were interrupted by the ringing of the phone. Liza reached for it impulsively; then remembering where she was, waited for Clare to answer.

"Yes, I know right where you can reach Liza. She's here with me." Covering the mouthpiece, she whispered, "It's Martha Newman!" She couldn't have looked more surprised.

Liza's mouth went dry, and the hand that reached for the phone trembled slightly. Martha wouldn't call her unless something had happened. "Hello, Martha. What is it?"

She thought she heard a trace of her

188

own anxiety in Martha's voice. "I think you're a friend of Bobby Harper, the man with whom Dr. Peterson is sailing. You didn't happen to hear from him today, did you?"

"I haven't heard anything." She kept her voice calm and friendly, even when she said, "But neither of them would necessarily be calling me. Did you expect to hear . . . "

"Yes, I expected a call from Dr. Peterson this morning."

We mustn't panic, Liza thought. It's too soon to call the Coast Guard. We don't know enough. "Was Dr. Peterson definite about phoning you this morning?"

"Yes, it was important . . . We had plans . . . "

Liza knew she couldn't wait passively any longer. "I can make some calls and let you know what I find."

Clare agreed that the night they had talked about the trip with Bobby in the restaurant, he had mentioned the marina where SONGSTRESS was berthed, but neither of them could remember its name. Finally, they called Simon at work, and he immediately came up with the name of a boatyard in Margate.

When he heard why they needed the name, he was frankly concerned. He urged Liza to call the Coast Guard if she found they had actually left the marina on Saturday morning.

"That's over forty-eight hours ago. They could swim to Calais in that time."

"Don't talk about swimming," Clare moaned.

A call to the boatyard revealed that SONGSTRESS had left her berth before the office opened on Saturday morning; that would be sometime before eight.

While Clare talked, Liza jotted notes on the description and probable route of the yacht and looked up the number for the Coast Guard.

The man who took her information did so with maddening equanimity.

He asked for her phone number, said they'd call if they had anything for her and hung up.

Clare put her arm around Liza and murmured, "They'll be all right. Don't think about the storm. Think about how strong and competent Dr. Peterson and Bobby are. Storms happen all the time."

The Coast Guard phoned back in twenty minutes to say an enquiry about the Yacht SONGSTRESS had been made by J. R. Harper, of St. Omer, France at ten Sunday night. Since then, they had been trying to contact the missing yacht by radio, but so far without success.

"The missing yacht!" Liza sobbed, hearing echoes from the past. "How horrible that sounds!"

9

NUMBLY, Liza accepted a cup of tea from Clare, who asked, "Should we tell Martha what we've learned?"

"I've been wondering the same thing. Which is worse — to hear no news, or to hear that the Coast Guard had already begun a search?"

"Let's wait a while," Clare advised.

Liza agreed. "Will you give me some jobs to do for you tonight, please? I can't sit still, and I know I won't be able to sleep."

"There's always wallpaper to peel and paint to strip."

She showed Liza where the tools were and found her a pair of heavy rubber gloves. "Watch out for this paint remover. Keep a window open when you use it or it rots your liver."

After going through the motions of

cooking a meal neither of them wanted, Clare prepared to leave for work. She gave Liza a few final instructions, and then, seeing a post card propped on the mantel, she said, "I almost forgot. Here — read this."

"From North Yemen!" Liza exclaimed. "Whom do we know . . . ?"

The message was written in a script that surpassed Andrews's for illegibility. She frowned, and Clare took back the card.

"It's from my cousin. He's made a quick trip out there and wants to stay with me Friday night on his way home. He doesn't know about the party, but I'm sure he'll enjoy it."

"Is this your Liverpool cousin?"

"Yes, and he's written that he's seen your application for the course. He hopes he'll have a chance to talk to you; so there's something you can be happy about."

Standing in the open doorway, Clare asked, "What shall I say at work? Martha will be around. She'll ask me if we've heard anything."

Liza had thought of this. Nurse Daniels might also ask questions. Reluctantly she decided she'd have to talk to Martha.

"If she asks what we've heard, tell her to ring me. Maybe by then I'll have some good news. And if Nurse Daniels asks, tell her we'll let her know whatever we learn. I hope there won't be a lot of talk . . . " She turned away as her voice broke.

Clare gave her a quick hug. "Liza dear, they'll be all right. Try not to worry."

From the second floor window, Liza watched her friend hurry toward her car. Before getting in she looked up and waved.

She's as worried as I am, Liza thought. But she doesn't have a load of guilt to add to her worry. If only I'd told Bobby I wanted to go and that I didn't want Andrew along. He'd have thought it odd, but he'd accept it.

When the phone rang, it was Martha,

and Liza's voice must have betrayed the anxiety she felt, because she said, "You don't sound like you have good news."

"Maybe no news is good news. Have you seen Clare?"

"I was waiting for her when she arrived. She told me to call you."

"We've learned from the Coast Guard that Bobby Harper's uncle in France had already contacted them, so everything is moving along."

Liza tried to think of something hopeful to say. "Dr. Peterson could just turn up there. He's on duty tonight, isn't he?" She knew this sounded unconvincing, but Martha went along with the act.

"Until he does, the registrar is covering for him. He was on second call."

Liza said, "The Coast Guard will call me, if they have news; but Dr. Peterson is more likely to get in touch with you. Will you let me know if you hear anything?"

Martha promised, saying, "Meanwhile, try not to worry. I have a hunch they're fine, and my hunches are often right."

She's so brave, Liza thought. How could I harbour such unkind feelings toward her. In her mind's eye, she saw Martha and Andrew talking together in the dining room on his first night at St. Anne's. How happy they looked together; and now she understood why — he gave her the feeling of importance she badly needed.

But what did Martha give him that kept him so attentive? Was it only the memory of the girl he had loved, or did he value her in her own right?

"The girl he had loved!" Liza realized this was wrong. Hadn't he told her he'd never been in love?

So, it must be that Martha is his real love, instead of a substitute for Flora! If only it isn't too late to see him and Martha together again, and then carry on the way I had planned, independently and unattached.

Sitting in the darkening room, she tried to remember what she'd heard about sailing in the English Channel — fog, strong currents, short, high, choppy waves, sudden changes in conditions, crowded shipping lanes, a dangerous reef off the Normandy coast. It was best not to think about it.

She put on the lights, and seeing Clare's buckets and tools, remembered she had jobs to do.

She started stripping paint where Clare and Simon had left off the weekend before. Systematically working her way around the foyer, she kept at the unpleasant job until she ran out of newspapers a little after midnight. Meaning to rest a few minutes before looking for more papers, she sprawled on the sofa.

When she woke, the pearly light of daybreak was visible beyond the windows and the telephone was ringing. She groped awkwardly to answer.

"They're all right!" It was Clare.

"Both of them?"

"Yes, and SONGSTRESS, too. They've just been talking to us. They're fine."

Liza was weak with relief. She could think of nothing to say.

Clare said, "Don't you want to hear the details?"

"Yes, tell me."

"I'll give you to Martha. Dr.Peterson explained it to her."

"Hi, Liza. Clare told you all that matters. They're safe — with Bobby Harper's uncle. They'll be back tonight."

"What did they say happened?"

"I don't really understand about it, and I didn't care much what had happened once I knew they were all right." She paused, as though trying to remember what she'd heard. "Andrew said when the storm became bad, they had to lie a-hull, whatever that means."

Liza explained briefly. "They dropped sails, went below, battened the hatches and rode out the storm."

"Well, whatever." Martha continued, obviously doubtful about what actually went on. "Anyway, while they were doing that, they were blown way off course. They were up along the Dutch coast somewhere, and they didn't have charts for the area, so they were sort of lost, as I understand . . ."

"Why didn't they get on the radio and . . ."

"Oh yes, that was the other trouble. They could receive messages, but they couldn't transmit, for some reason. So they knew the Coast Guard was looking for them, but they couldn't tell them they were safe.

"It took all this time to get sorted out because the wind was from the wrong direction, and they ran out of fuel for their engine." Martha sighed. "Isn't it lovely to know they're fine!"

Shedding tears of joy, Liza cleaned up her stripping mess from the night before; and by the time Clare turned up with a box of jam doughnuts for a celebration breakfast, she'd had a shower and dressed.

Both girls were suddenly starving. When the last doughnut crumb was gone, Liza said, "Do you know, Andrew and Bobby would be amazed if they knew how you and I have been agonizing over them."

Clare looked puzzled.

"Neither of them would expect us to know they were missing."

"What are you getting at?"

"Only that I'm celebrating the return of two sailors whom I was never going to see again, anyway."

"Don't be silly," Clare admonished. "You're going to see both of them. They're coming to the party on Friday to celebrate their deliverance. I asked Martha, too. I hope you don't mind. I know how . . . "

"Of course I don't mind." Liza hid her consternation by going for more coffee. She had been preparing herself to go through life without ever again seeing Andrew.

A few more days of painting and papering, a day of cooking and baking, and it was party day.

The Liverpool cousin arrived during the final count-down, catching Clare in the shower and Liza, half dressed, roaming around looking for her hair dryer.

She grabbed a bath robe and let in a vastly overweight, middle-aged man, still puffing from climbing the stairs.

Clare, soaking wet, put her head around the bathroom door. "Percy! How marvellous!"

She introduced Liza to the man they hoped might put her career back on the tracks.

"Aha," said Percy. "I've seen your application for our course. We must talk. The whole situation has changed."

Wouldn't it just, Liza thought. Ah well, she'd never been wild about the idea of going back to college. In any event, the talking had to wait; for, as Clare announced to her cousin — some thirty guests would be arriving within the hour.

Simon came in with an armful of bottles and a stained and ragged photocopy of a punch recipe, guaranteed by his boss to warm the cockles of the coldest heart. Though he and Percy had not met before, they made a good team.

"We'll take care of everything," Simon assured the girls. "You make yourselves beautiful."

Liza looked critically at her reflection in Clare's full length mirror, wishing she had something simpler than her jade silk dress. With her three inch heels, it created the wrong effect — as though she were trying too hard to look glamorous, but it was her only party dress.

The thought of seeing Andrew again made her feel tense and breathless.

Clare walked through her freshly decorated rooms, looked at the platters of party food in the kitchen, went back into the living room where her fiancé, her best friend and her favourite cousin stood around a bit stiffly and expectantly; and she threw herself into Simon's arms, sobbing, "I'm too happy."

The doorbell rang, and the party began.

Liza knew most of the guests. Nearly everyone from Casualty was going to stop by, even if they couldn't stay.

The flat filled quickly. Liza was aware that Andrew had not yet appeared by nine o'clock. Will I be glad or sorry if he doesn't come? She tried to believe she didn't care.

She was chatting with Percy just as Andrew and Martha arrived. She looked away quickly.

Seeing Andrew in the doorway, Percy said, "By George! It can't be. But it is!"

He handed Liza his tray of glasses, and she watched him push through the crowd, which separated quickly before his great bulk. His right hand pumped Andrew's, while his left thumped his shoulder. She saw Andrew's delighted response.

He finally introduced Martha, who looked heart-breakingly beautiful in a white wool dress with a dark blue scarf that perfectly matched her eyes.

Liza carried Percy's tray of empty glasses into the kitchenette where she filled the sink with hot water and accidently squeezed in far too much soap. She felt so tense, she hardly dared touch Clare's fragile glasses.

Simon joined her and started drying; standing with his back to the sink, he said, "It's a good party. I thought it would be. Clare never fails . . . " He left his sentence unfinished. "There's Bobby."

He waved, and they both made their way to the door to greet the drummer who knew only a few of the other guests.

Bobby's account of his sailing adventure was brief, and to Liza's disappointment, included nothing about Andrew or how they got along together.

"And now you'll be off to Australia?"

"In three days."

Clare interrupted them to ask Liza, "Do you think people want to dance? Shall I put on some music?"

Bobby said, "Let's see what you have," and headed eagerly toward her music centre.

Clare left him in charge, and he began sorting through her tapes, handing Liza his choices.

When the dancing began, he led her onto the floor. She had never danced with anyone as good as Bobby. He made her feel that she was hardly touching the floor.

Andrew and Martha were dancing nearby, and Andrew's eyes met hers for just a moment, but it was almost as though he had looked through her.

She hid her face against Bobby's shoulder. He's completely besotted with Martha, she thought forlornly. But I prayed that I'd see them together again;

I'm seeing a prayer answered. I should be happy.

Bobby had to leave early. He briskly hugged Liza and Clare, muttering that he didn't want to go, but it was just another work night for him.

"I hate goodbyes. Maybe I'll see you after Australia. Cheerio."

Liza was in the foyer when, around midnight, Andrew and Martha were leaving. Martha sounded genuinely friendly when she said, "We never did have a chance to chat. But isn't it a nice party?"

Andrew, standing beside her, was apparently going to ignore Liza, as he had done all evening, but Martha said, "Wait. I've forgotten my bag."

He was left face to face with Liza.

I'm not going to turn and run, she resolved; and smiling, she said, "I've never thanked you for sparing me a rather uncomfortable sail."

Without returning her smile, he said, "If it were only the discomfort, I might have left you to it."

Here we go again, she thought. "From what fate worse than discomfort did you think you were saving me?"

Andrew took a step closer and said, "Liza, I'm sure you know how I feel about you throwing yourself at a married man, though I realize I have no influence."

Furious that he'd ignored her explanation of her relationship with Bobby, deeply hurt that he'd bring this up when they were supposed to be enjoying a party, Liza felt her self control abandon her.

"A man who would marry without love, shouldn't sound so self righteous," she retorted.

He looked stunned for just a second, going so pale, the scar on his forehead suddenly stood out vividly. Then hiding any feeling, he said, "Liza, what are you talking about. I never . . . "

"No, you never — because Flora died."

The terrible words were out, and they could never be taken back. What was worse, Martha had returned and must have heard, for she said to Andrew, "What's this all about?"

"Nothing, Martha. Nurse Carter is a little confused." He took her arm and they left.

Liza watched them go, unable for a while to make a move. It wasn't Andrew's words that dried up the blood in her veins. It was the way he looked at her, as though he despised her. She fled to the only refuge in the crowded little flat — the bathroom.

She hid her face in her hands. He has every right to hate me, she thought.

Someone rattled the door knob. She quickly washed her burning face and returned to the party.

It lasted until after two; and when the last guest had gone, Clare kicked off her shoes and collapsed on the sofa. "Was it all right, do you suppose?" she asked.

"It was the best ever," Simon exclaimed.

"I certainly picked the right night to

be in London," Percy observed.

For Liza, it had not been a great party, but Clare would never know that. She smiled at her friend. "You're a perfect hostess, Clare."

Since Liza occupied the only guest room, Simon took Percy home with him; but the two men turned up Saturday morning for a late breakfast.

While Clare and Simon dawdled over second and third cups of coffee, enjoying a post-mortem of the party, Percy took Liza aside and said, "Sit down. I'm afraid I'm going to try to talk you out of taking that course."

So, Liza thought, I didn't send in my application soon enough, and there are no places left. Clare had urged her to get her application in.

"You know," Percy continued, "I'm just back from North Yemen."

"Yes, I wanted to hear about it."

"It's what I want to tell you about. Where do I start? Do you know where it is?"

"Somewhere in the Middle East?"

"Right. It's in what's called 'The Empty Quarter' of the Arabian Peninsula." He paused, as though to gauge Liza's interest.

"Roads throughout the country are primitive. And isolated hospitals and clinics with limited resources have catchment areas of hundreds of square kilometres."

"It sounds so much like what my grandmother wrote about Assam fifty years ago!" Liza exclaimed.

"There's a great deal to be done." Percy listed some of the problems of the area. "In the clinics, they not only deal with routine cases but with malaria and typhoid. Malnutrition, measles and whooping cough keep the infant mortality high. And you can imagine the problems the midwives face. So, that's the general picture."

Liza, sitting on the edge of her chair, so intent upon what he was saying, she hardly remembered to breathe, asked, "What were you doing there?"

"I've been appointed to recruit and

train staff for the agencies operating in such areas. It's important for me to see, at first hand, the kind of places our trainees will be sent when they finish the course. This was my first trip."

"And you went to those isolated parts?"

"I went to a village at the end of the most unbelievable eight hour drive through the mountains. There, a small clinic serves a population of about fifty thousand, spread over a hundred square kilometres. One Sudanese doctor runs it with the help of a part-time Yemeni doctor. There are two nurses and a midwife from the Netherlands.

"None of this team has had a holiday in over a year. The midwife is on the verge of a break-down. But there's no one to relieve them."

"How can that be?" Liza found it hard to believe the world wasn't full of people who would jump at this challenge.

"So many of those who would

normally relieve them — people trained and accustomed to this kind of work — have been diverted to the famine areas in Africa. There aren't enough to go around. That's why we're starting the course you applied for."

"So, why didn't you want to take me?"

"Because I'd like you to go to North Yemen without taking the course."

"I'll go. Of course, I'll go." She couldn't sit still. Rising from her chair, she paced to the window and back. "I'm ready to leave any time — tomorrow!"

Clare, seeing Liza pace about the room, called, "What's going on over there, some kind of mini-marathon?"

"Doesn't Clare know about this?" Liza asked.

"We've been too busy with the party to talk."

"Come on then, let's tell her."

When Percy described Liza's destination, Simon looked worried. "Liza, why go to such a place? It sounds absolutely awful!"

She didn't know how to explain that the very awfulness was the reason she wanted to go. It would sound pretty ridiculous.

"I've always wanted to work in that sort of place." She knew it was a lame answer, and was grateful to Simon for not pursuing the question.

Their leisurely breakfast ended suddenly when Percy said, "Look at the time! I'll miss my train!"

"Can't we drive you part way?" Clare asked.

She and Simon were about to set off for Cumbria, but Percy said he already had his ticket and he planned to finish a report on the train. "You could drop me off at the station, though. You'll be going past it."

"Would you drop me off at the library," Liza asked.

She had everything to learn about North Yemen, and knowing the libraries closed at five on Saturdays, she didn't want to lose a minute.

"I must give you my spare key." Clare told her, as they prepared to leave.

Percy gave her his office phone number with instructions to call him Monday afternoon. She carefully tucked it into her wallet, which also held her precious passport; and after taking out her library card and a pound note, put the wallet safely away in her room. She checked that she had a pen and notebook in her bag and put on an old jacket.

"Did you say you already have your cholera immunization?" Percy asked her.

"Right. I was all set to go to Assam whenever they wanted me."

"Remember," Clare called from her bedroom, "You don't leave the country before the wedding. Percy, you see to it."

As they bustled about, Simon quickly cleared away the breakfast things. Clare checked her kitchen before leaving, saying, "Liza, please eat some of this food while we're away. By Monday night it will be getting on a bit."

As steeple bells were chiming six, Liza turned down Clare's street, burdened with an armful of books and a carton of milk and knowing much more about North Yemen than she'd known when she set out.

Half way up the stairs she thought, where did I put Clare's key? By the time she reached the door to the flat, she knew. She hadn't put it anywhere. Clare had forgotten, in all the rush, to give it to her.

Not wanting to believe this, she put down her pile of books and her pint of milk and combed through every nook and cranny of her bag. No key.

Fortunately, she knew Clare left a spare key with an old woman across the hall. She rang that bell and waited hopefully. The woman was out. There was nothing to do but wait for her return. She walked to the park and back. Then she did it again. Maybe she's away for the weekend!

Sitting at the top of the staircase, she pondered her predicament. She counted her change — forty pence, and went through her bag, auditing her resources. A comb, a notebook, used tissues, half of a chocolate bar, her pen, a wad of brochures she had picked up in the library. That was it. Everything else was safely locked away on the other side of Clare's door.

I'll go to St. Anne's and beg Matron to let me use my old room just one night, she decided. No other possibility presented itself.

Next, she was faced with the choice of spending ten pence, a quarter of her working capital, on a phone call to first ask Matron if her room was empty, or splashing out and spending everything on bus fare to the hospital. There really was no choice, because if she spent the money on the telephone there wouldn't be enough for the bus.

Matron was sympathetic, but she said, "I'm sorry, there's a course on.

Every room is assigned."

Liza's mournful sigh must have touched her heart, for she said, "Perhaps, if you go over and ask someone who's on duty tonight, they'd give you their key. We could get you some sheets."

"Oh, thank you, Matron." She was sure Nurse Daniels would come to the rescue and hurried across the courtyard. It was getting late.

As she approached Casualty, she slowed her pace. She couldn't face Andrew or Martha. She peered through the doors. For a Saturday night it looked very quiet.

There was no one in sight except the night sister, an older woman Liza hardly knew, since she and Clare always worked the same rota. She slipped through the doors. The waiting room was empty.

The sister didn't recognize her out of uniform.

"Sorry," she said. "Nurse Daniels is on holiday until after Easter. Could someone else help you?"

Liza glanced at the clock. It was after eleven! Suddenly her situation seemed hopeless.

Despairingly, she thought, I don't really belong anywhere. I can't walk the streets all night. What becomes of people like me?

Sister looked concerned but a little impatient. "Can't someone else help you tonight?"

It would be too humiliating to tell this woman, "I used to work here and I'm looking for a place to doss down for the night."

"May I sit in the waiting room a few minutes, please?" Without waiting for an answer, she hurried into the empty room and slumped into a chair, her library books piled on her lap. She was as far out of sight from the entry as possible.

If people would leave me alone, she thought, I could stay here until I get a better idea. She closed her eyes to think.

"Is something wrong, Nurse Carter? Are you ill?"

She woke with a start. The last person in the world she wanted to see was standing over her.

10

IT was the totally unexpected kindness in Andrew's voice that opened the floodgates. Tears sprang to her eyes. She hid her face in her hands and wept.

In a tiny voice, she managed to say, "Nothing is wrong. I just have no place to go."

"Must you go someplace?"

"I mean no place to sleep. I'm locked out everywhere."

"Clare locked you out?" Andrew's tone was incredulous.

Liza shook her head.

A puzzled frown wrinkled the doctor's brow. "Is it Bobby Harper? Did he lock you out?"

"Why didn't I think of him!" Liza exclaimed. "He would — " Too late, she noticed Andrew's reaction.

"Yes, why didn't you go to him for help?"

"I don't have any money, and I don't know where he lives."

Liza blew her nose mightily. On second thought, Bobby wasn't such a good solution. He'd probably be out drumming somewhere. And now, she had angered Andrew again, just by considering him.

He still stood over her, looking half annoyed and half mystified. At last, he said, "Liza, if you had a place to sleep right now, would that be any help?"

"It's all I need," she sobbed.

"Come with me." He took her library books from her.

She followed him through the silent, half-lit corridors, hardly noticing where he was leading her. At the end of a short cul-de-sac he reached into his pocket for a key, opened a door and snapped on the light.

"The loo is around the corner. Try not to be seen and don't lock yourself out."

He left her, and with the closing of the door, her tears began again. He was so kind. It was so humiliating to receive good for evil.

She took off her shoes and lay on top of the bedspread using her jacket for a cover. The room was warm and quiet. Her last thought before falling into deep slumber was, this must be where Andrew sleeps.

Brilliant sunlight woke her a little after seven. She lay very still trying to remember where she was. It all came back to her at once, and she sat up, appalled at the memory of what had happened the night before.

I'll get out of here before Andrew comes back, she thought, but I must thank him for rescuing me. She dug her notebook and a pen from the bottom of her bag and wrote a short note.

Propping it where he'd surely find it, she discovered Andrew had, indeed, put her into his own room, for she saw, sparkling in the sunlight on the dresser, the quartz pebble from the little pool beneath the waterfall.

"For remembering until we come

back again," he had said when he picked it up.

But she had freed him of his promise to return. Why hadn't he thrown away the pebble?

She heard a light tapping at the door and then the jingle of keys. Feeling guilty about snooping, she quickly lay down again before Andrew entered.

He sat beside her, and said very quietly, "We'd better get you out of here while there's no one around, but first I want to talk to you."

He rose and walked to the window where he stood with his hands in his pockets, rattling coins. "You didn't think of going to Bobby Harper last night?"

"Not until you mentioned him."

Liza wished they could go to the dining room to talk. She was starving.

"And you don't know where Bobby lives?"

"Someplace in Chelsea, I think . . . "

Andrew interrupted her. "Liza, I've been thinking about you two. I'm really confused. But there is something I must be sure you know."

He made her wait while he seemed to ponder what he would say. "Bobby and I had a lot of time to talk, as you know. He told me about a personal problem. I'm violating his confidence now, but I want you to know this before you become too deeply involved with him."

"Not only is he married which, I take it, you've known right along, but he has no intention of ever divorcing his wife. He has no thought of — " He stopped, perturbed at Liza's amused expression.

"No thought of making an honest woman of me? Andrew, I know."

"And that doesn't matter to you?" He stood over her, his eyes flashing.

"Not a bit."

He swooped upon her like a hawk, grasping her shoulders, shaking her. "Liza, you tramp!"

"Can't you understand? I've explained. We're just friends!"

"I'm supposed to believe that after

watching how you danced together?"

He was holding her down, glaring at her.

"Get off me, Andrew!" Her voice rang loud in the quiet room, and he clamped his hand over her mouth.

"Let me out of here." She tried to roll off the bed. "Why do you refuse to see . . . "

"Will you be quiet?" His voice was a snarl.

Suddenly, violently, he covered her mouth with his, but a moment later the fury and cruelty of his kiss vanished. His lips became gentle. His hands, which had held her down so harshly, released their grip and caressed her, leaving tracks of fire on her skin. His breath came hot and ragged.

Fighting an almost overpowering compulsion to respond lovingly, she forced herself to remember this was the man who belonged to Martha.

Yet it was her own name he spoke over and over in a voice that throbbed with love. Her resistance broke. She couldn't deny the force that drew them together, nor it seemed, could he.

Lying with her arms around him, she wanted to hold him close forever. It seemed the only way they could show each other how they truly felt.

Words always failed them. The quartz pebble, still on the dresser, revealed more to Liza than Andrew's words could ever tell.

Finally, he pulled himself free, rising in one swift motion to stand at the window, his back to her.

"What are we doing, Liza? I simply don't know. You're driving me crazy."

He broke off, listening. They both remained silent, hardly breathing, as footsteps sounded beyond his door. There was the click of a lock and a door opened and closed.

Liza sat up and leaned against the wall. Nurses weren't even allowed in this corridor. She must leave before they created a scandal.

Rising quickly, she lurched against the door, dizzy and light-headed.

Andrew was at her side immediately to put an arm around her and support her as she sat down again.

"I forgot. I didn't eat yesterday," she explained.

He looked at his watch. "In a few minutes we can go down and get some breakfast."

"I'd love that."

"Meanwhile, tell me what happened last night — who turned you out. I still don't know how you wound up so pathetically waif-like in Casualty."

"Clare forgot to give me a key, or I forgot to get it from her, but there are much more important things to talk about now."

She needed to know how he felt about what had just happened to them. What did these tempestuous embraces mean to him? She didn't know how to ask.

What about Martha?

Aside from this tangle of relationships, there were other questions. She was desperate to tell him about the job in North Yemen and to find out what he would do, now that his brother-in-law had solved the family problems in Springbeck.

But there was one matter that must be settled once and for all before they left the room.

"Sit with me a minute." She spoke just above a whisper.

He joined her on the edge of the bed.

"For the record, and for the last time: I don't care that Bobby Harper is married and plans to stay married because there is nothing between him and me but friendship."

"You don't have to explain anything to me Liza."

"I do have to explain, so we'll never quarrel about this again. Your disapproving attitude . . . "

"I was only afraid you'd be hurt."

"But you don't mind hurting me."

He turned to face her, frowning, waiting for her to go on. When she didn't, he went back to the subject of Bobby.

"You keep saying you and Bobby are just friends, but your actions, right along and as recently as Clare's party, lead me to think differently. You seem to be throwing yourself at him. Everybody has talked about it."

"You sound so pompous and self righteous when you talk about Bobby and me. I can't believe you take hospital gossip seriously. If you prefer to accept what you hear, I can't help it. But I'll tell you something Bobby and I have that you and I have never had — a lot of real understanding."

Andrew glared at her. "So, he understands you, but I hurt you."

"You must be aware of that. How can you expect to juggle my heart and Martha's without breaking one of them?"

His hand covered hers as she fidgeted with a well-shredded tissue. "If I've hurt you, Liza, I'm sorry." His voice was grave.

She knew he was sincere, but felt he wasn't certain what this apology was supposed to cover.

"You aren't innocent of causing pain, yourself," he added.

It came to her in a flash — how could she speak of causing pain! It was he who was owed an apology. Her cruel remark about marrying someone he didn't love had been made deliberately. She'd wanted to cause as much pain as she knew how.

She turned to face him. "What I said about you and Flora . . . "

He wasn't going to make it easy for her. He waited, showing no emotion.

"You once told me you had never been in love. Do you remember?"

He nodded. She hoped he didn't remember how she had blatantly asked him if he'd been in love, even before they knew each other very well.

"Your mother told me, that same day, about your engagement. I was shocked that you would have married without love. But I had no right to mention it — ever."

Andrew said, "A little knowledge can be a dangerous thing."

They sat in silence a few minutes. Then he said, "The day we drove back from Springbeck together I wanted to tell you something no other living person knows, but we talked about different things, as it turned out, and after that . . . I didn't think you'd be interested."

Liza remembered how, on that trip through the rainy countryside, she had nagged him about the foolishness of applying for his father's practice. What cheek! It wasn't strange he had chosen to say little after that.

He said, "I began to suspect your interest was less in me than in the foreign job you hoped I could get for you."

"Oh, Andrew! I suspected your main interest in me was to find a nurse to work in Springbeck."

"If I had told you then about Flora and about poor Martha, you would have understood what I've tried to do. It wasn't fair of me to ask for trust . . . "

"That day on the stairs! What did you mean?"

"It's a long story, Liza." He looked at his watch. "Put on your shoes. We have to get out of here or you're sure to be seen. We'll talk at breakfast."

Reluctantly, she slipped into her shoes. "This is the cause of half our trouble," she complained. "We've never had enough time to talk!"

As they approached the dining room, the smell of food banished all other thoughts from Liza's mind. She loaded her tray and then remembered she had no money.

"Oh, Andrew!"

"I know," he said, reaching into his pocket. "You're my guest today."

He led her to a table at the back of the room.

"My library books," she gasped. "I left them in your room."

Without a word, he put down his tray and left.

Sitting alone, dressed in her old jacket and slacks, she felt out of place, and looking around, she didn't see a familiar face until Andrew returned with her books.

Directly behind him came the Nursing Supervisor who noticed Liza immediately and headed toward her.

"Nurse Carter, may I see you in my office, please?"

Liza felt herself go pale. "Of course, Mrs. Headly." Now I'm in for it, she thought, rising to follow the older woman.

"After your breakfast will be soon enough. There's no rush."

When the supervisor was beyond hearing, Liza turned to Andrew who was examining the pile of books. "Someone must have seen me in your corridor," she moaned.

"Impossible. I was watching. Stop worrying and eat."

She had forced herself to wait politely for his return and didn't have to be told twice to begin.

"Why the sudden interest in North Yemen" he asked, shoving her books aside and tackling his ham and eggs.

He glanced up and saw joy suddenly sparkling in her eyes. "It just happens I'm going there any day now!"

"We certainly do have a lot to talk about."

"First tell me what you started to tell me — " she lowered her voice, "In your room."

"Yes." He put down his fork and knife and gave her his full attention. "There are two things you must be told, one of them you should have known, in fact, long ago."

He looked up and swore under his breath. Liza followed his gaze and saw a frail, little, white-coated doctor approaching.

"May I join you, Dr. Peterson?" the man lowered his tray onto their table without waiting for an answer.

With her eyes, Liza implored Andrew to send him away. This might be their last chance to talk. But he politely introduced Dr. Dixon, and all Liza could do was grit her teeth and smile back at the little man.

He was still with them when they left the dining room, and he continued down the corridor with Andrew after Liza turned off to go to the Supervisor's office. Andrew said nothing about meeting her afterward.

A student nurse came out of the inner office, her face flushed, looking neither to the right or left. Oh dear me, Liza shuddered. It's a bad morning at St. Anne's.

"Yes, come in, Nurse Carter. Sit down." The calm controlled voice of the Supervisor gave nothing away. "Nurse Carter, I don't believe you are employed in this hospital at present."

"No, Mrs. Headly." Liza thought simple, yes-or-no answers would be safest.

"So you are visiting this morning?"

"Yes, Mrs. Headly."

"And are you employed elsewhere?"

"I'm waiting to hear about a position

for which I've applied."

"Ah, in that case, I wonder if you could resume your locum for a few days. That poor girl who came back from maternity leave last week has produced a pair of sleepless twins. She needs a bit more time to get them regulated."

Liza could hardly hide her relief. "When would you like me to start?"

"Could you come in tonight?"

She was about to agree when she remembered she might still be locked out if Clare came home late. "I might have a problem about a uniform." She hoped she wouldn't have to explain.

"Otherwise you'd be willing to come in tonight?"

"I'd be very happy to, Mrs. Headly."

The Supervisor was confident that, if necessary, a uniform could be found. She lifted her phone, called the Matron and informed her that Nurse Carter would need a room.

Liza held her breath while Mrs. Headly listened briefly.

"Nonsense, of course you have a

room." After another short wait, she said, "Lovely, Matron. Thank you. She'll be right over."

Andrew had been heading toward Casualty with Dr. Dixon, and it was in that direction that Liza turned when she left the Supervisor's office.

Searching for him, she became aware that, without her uniform, she looked suspicious, peeking into the doctor's room and into Ward C where the nurse collecting breakfast trays asked, "Can I help you, Miss?"

"I'm looking for Dr. Peterson. He doesn't seem to be around."

The day sister said, "I think he's signed out. Just let me look."

He was gone, signed out to Dr. Dixon who was busy with a patient.

Completely frustrated, Liza decided it was up to him to find her if he had anything to say. But she couldn't stop wondering what he was talking about when he'd said: "There are two things you must be told — things you should have known long ago."

★ ★ ★

She moved back into the residence with no other luggage than her pile of library books and passed the morning poring over them, blissfully contemplating the adventure she'd be launching upon in the near future. How near, she didn't realize until the afternoon.

With change borrowed from the student midwife, she tried unsuccessfully to phone Clare, and then, through the operator, tried to reach Percy, whose number was safely tucked away in her wallet behind Clare's locked door.

When the University exchange managed to track him down, he said, "Liza, I've been ringing you at Clare's all morning."

"But you told me to phone you in the afternoon."

"Yes, but something has come up."

Liza's heart sank. "What happened?"

"They rang me from North Yemen this morning. They'd like you to start as quickly as possible. Can you leave

238

on Friday morning?"

"Friday morning? This Friday morning?"

"I know this is sudden, but it would be very helpful if you could arrange to go that soon."

He waited for a response, but none came. "Liza, are you there? Hello?"

"I'm here, in a state of shock! Of course, I can leave on Friday."

"Good. This morning I posted various papers and bits of information you'll need. Your contract and your new postal address are included. You'll pick up your tickets and travel documents at the airport. Call me if you have any questions in the meanwhile."

Dazed, Liza returned to her room. I must make lists, she thought, and then she remembered Clare's wedding. She'd miss it, after all.

She tried Clare's number every half hour, and in between, ravenously gleaned information from the books, marvelling that by the end of the week, she would enter the totally alien world she was reading about.

At three, Clare answered her phone on the first ring. "We just now walked in," she exclaimed. "Everything took longer than we expected, but I'm back in time to go on duty tonight."

Trying to make a joke of it, Liza told her she'd been caught out without a key.

Clare was appalled. "You poor lamb! How could I do such a thing! What did you do?"

Without going into detail, Liza told her she'd gone back to the residence and would be working a few more days at her old job, which delighted Clare; but news that she'd leave for North Yemen on Friday didn't please her at all.

"How could Percy do this to me! Can't you put off leaving until after the wedding? It's only a fortnight."

"I wouldn't miss your wedding for anything else." Liza explained. "But Percy really considers this urgent. And you know I'll be with you in spirit."

Clare was only partially mollified. "It will be fun working together a few more nights, anyway. I'm going to miss you awfully."

Clare was already at her desk, looking as calm and controlled as ever when Liza reported for duty. There was no time to talk.

Liza was sent off to X-Ray with a patient who didn't know a word of English. This is what it will be like most of the time after Friday, she thought.

From X-Ray her patient was sent to the plaster room and Liza was kept busy there during a little rush early in the evening, but by ten, the waiting room was empty, and she and Clare seemed to be all that was left of the staff.

"Where is everybody?" she asked. "Are we short-handed?"

"Nurse Daniels is on holiday. Martha finished her module, and the students have their prelims tomorrow."

Without even mentioning Andrew's absence, she launched into the story of her trip to Willowbrook. She described her wedding plans in such detail that Liza visualized clearly the ceremony she'd have to miss in the little school chapel.

It wasn't until they went on their break that Clare turned to her friend and exclaimed, "I haven't given you a chance to say a word about your adventure. You're going on Friday. Can you possibly be ready?"

"It's amazingly easy. Percy is taking care of all the details.

She stopped short to peer into the corridor where she thought she saw Andrew. It was someone else. She decided to end the suspense. "Clare, where's Andrew tonight?"

Her friend's look of surprise alarmed her. "Didn't you know? He finished this weekend. Dr. Dixon has taken his place."

Liza couldn't conceal her disappointment. "But he was here this morning. I saw him. He didn't say anything about leaving. He didn't even . . . say goodbye. Do you know where he went?"

"I suppose to Springbeck, but I don't know."

Liza couldn't believe he was gone. Now he'd never know she finally set off on her foreign job, and she would never know what he was about to tell her when Dr. Dixon interrupted their breakfast conversation.

She worked only two nights before moving back with Clare to do her final shopping and packing. They were having tea on Thursday night when a long distance call came for her.

"I can pick you up at six tomorrow morning and drive you to the airport, right?"

It was Andrew!

"That's wonderful, but . . . " She could hardly speak.

"Good. See you then."

"Where is he?" Clare asked.

Liza shrugged. "How does he know I'm going away tomorrow?" she asked, and her friend shrugged.

"He's a strange man," Clare remarked.

"That about sums him up." True to his word, he rang the bell at six.

Liza looked down into the street and saw the green Morgan double parked. It was raining. Her luggage would be soaked on the little rack at the back of the car. While she watched, a second car parked behind Andrew's.

She heard him on the stairs and ran to let him in.

He picked up her case. She hugged Clare, wiped her eyes, and followed him.

In the street he astonished her by shoving her case into the car behind his. "To keep it dry," he said. "Come on."

Bewildered, she climbed into the familiar little car. "Who is that behind us?" she demanded.

"Friends of mine. Don't worry." He shifted into high and took her hand. "So, you're on your way, Nurse Carter. Are you happy?"

"Divinely. But how did you know?"

"Percy told me. And I had those two

244

things to tell you yet, so I thought I'd run you to your plane."

The rain fell harder. At top speed, the wipers barely cleared the small windscreen. The side windows steamed up, and Liza felt cozily isolated from the world in the intimate little space she shared with Andrew.

When they stopped for traffic lights, he turned to her and said, "I'll tell you now what I should have told you that first time we rode together in the rain. It's sad, and I'll make it short."

He spoke rapidly and in a monotone, never glancing from the road. "My parents and Flora's were friends, and we were considered to be childhood sweethearts, though in medical college we drifted apart.

"Then in a terrible accident, her parents were killed, and she was badly hurt. After that, she became very dependent upon me, and she begged me to take her with me to Africa.

"We were engaged, and I sent for her

as soon as I was settled. It was the worst thing I could have done. She became so depressed, she'd go days without speaking."

The traffic lights changed. He put the car in gear and continued.

"One night, after a particularly bad time, I suggested she should go to London for treatment. This upset her so badly, I didn't dare leave her alone, but she slipped out, and in the clinic's only Land Rover, she headed into the jungle. We found her two days later where a bridge had been blown up.

"Neither my parents nor Martha knew how badly things went in Africa before Flora ran away. Martha remembers her sister as the cheerful, lively girl she'd known before her parents were killed.

"When I arrived at St. Anne's and looked her up she attached herself to me as her last link with any of her family, as someone who still mourned her sister."

He paused. It seemed he was

wondering how to go on. Then in a different tone, as though he was asking for understanding, he said, "So, imagine her feelings if she should have to witness her dead sister's fiancé falling precipitously in love with another woman. It would be an impossible situation for her. But it's also impossible to turn off love."

He smiled at Liza who looked completely bewildered. "My first ploy was to send Martha to Paris so I could whisk you away to Springbeck. I had visions of settling you safely in Cumbria's mountain fastness and eventually joining you. But you had your own ideas, so after that, I tried, as you so aptly put it, to juggle the two of you. I foolishly asked you to trust me without explaining anything."

"Wait, Andrew." Liza's voice trembled. "I'm not sure I understand. You were falling in love with someone. I don't understand, with whom?"

"With you, of course, silly goose. Who else?"

"With me! Oh, Andrew!" She sobbed. "Why didn't you tell me. With all those passionate embraces, you never did."

"I was in no position to until Martha moved on, or one of us did. But I tried once to find out how you felt about us . . ."

"Is that what you meant when you asked me if I wanted you to keep your promise?"

"Yes."

"And I said no. I didn't mean no."

"I'm afraid I have a lot to learn about women."

They had reached the airport, and everything began happening too fast. Liza desperately wanted to sit still and talk, but Andrew's friends in the other car pulled alongside them.

While one handed Liza's case and a small leather folder to Andrew. The other took his place in the driver's seat of the Morgan. They drove the two cars away.

"Who are those men? Where are they going with your car? Andrew, what . . . ?" Liza stood in the rain, trying to make sense of what was happening.

"Not to worry." Andrew took her arm and led her into the terminal. As Percy had promised, her tickets were ready for her at the check-in desk. Her luggage was placed on the scales; she was given her boarding pass and told to proceed through Security to the departure lounge.

She turned to Andrew. "How can I go away from you now?" Tears streamed down her cheeks.

He wiped them away. "You could stay here, after all. Say you changed your mind."

"Then I wouldn't be worth your love. Do you understand?"

He nodded. "Remember, had two things to tell you."

"What's the other? Tell me quickly."

"I'm going with you," he declared.

"But how . . . "

"Didn't you know Percy needed a doctor, too?"

She hid her face against his broad chest and wept with joy. "But you can't," she sobbed.

"And why can't I?"

"Your car. You can't just . . ."

"I sold it yesterday to the gentleman who drove it away."

"Your luggage. You haven't any."

"It went by air freight on Tuesday, along with five cases of medicine and an autoclave."

He had opened the leather folder and was taking out plane tickets and his passport. They saw the attendant at the security gate beckoning Liza.

"Go along," Andrew said. "I'll be with you."

"Will you?" She let go his arm reluctantly. "Will you, always and forever?"

"Forever and wherever, my love."